ISBN: 9781951240967

Table of Contents

ACKNOWLEDGMENTS

I would like to acknowledge, as I so often do, the brilliant cover produced by Nick Deligaris and the skillful editing of Tammy Salyer.

Chapter 1

The little creature sniffed cautiously along the ground. It had been hours since she'd seen another living thing in this fringe of the desert. Normally, it would be a simple thing to spend days without encountering another soul, but in this moment, it was a hard-won achievement. Even if there wasn't a whisper or the tiniest whiff, she knew she was being followed.

She moved low along the sandy ground, testing the dry air and squinting at the setting sun through the wavy heat. Small, cunning paws gripped the shifting ground as she scampered into the shade of a dune. She sampled a breeze with her snout and pivoted her pointed ears. Nothing. Not a sound, not a scent. She swept her tail to and fro and tried to remain calm, but she couldn't. The giddiness was rising up in her. She'd done it. She'd actually done it. She'd slipped away, lost her pursuer. It couldn't be more than a few minutes before the sun would drop below the horizon, and then…

The sand behind her crunched, washing the giddiness away in a wave of panic. She didn't even waste the moment it would have taken to see what made the sound. She already knew. It was the same beast that had been following her since sunrise. She sprang forward in a desperate bid for escape, but her ragged shirt pulled tight, and she was left dangling just above the ground.

Her heart rattled in her chest as the creature turned her about. She came face-to-face with it, its sandy-gray eyes giving her a cold, measuring look. No amount of struggling could dislodge her from the clawed fingers that held her. Then, with a slow and deliberate motion, her captor reached out and grazed the clawed fingers of its other hand gently across the cream-colored fur of the little beast's throat.

"Slash," the hunter said. "Dead."

"That's not *fair*, Mama! How did you find me?" the little creature said, her tone more whiny than terrified.

"Do not say to me that it is not fair, Reyna." Her mother set the creature down and smoothed her fur. "Things will not be fair always. And they will *never* be fair unless you make them fair."

"And we don't make them fair," Reyna said, her eyes rolling and her voice taking on the singsong cadence of a piece of advice she'd heard a thousand times. "We make them unfair in our favor."

"That's right," her mother said, nodding. "Now tell me what it is you did not do that you should have done."

"I did *everything*," Reyna objected. "I knew *you* were over *there*, so I kept the wind on *that* side to blow my scent away from you. And I stayed low and moved between the tall places instead of over them. I did *everything*."

"Everything?" her mother asked, tapping her cloth-wrapped foot on the ground.

Reyna looked down and saw her own footprints and those of her mother's.

"Oh…"

"It is the easiest thing, Reyna. And the most dangerous. A man cannot smell you. His dogs can, but he cannot. And in the dark or from afar, a man cannot see you. But a man will always see what you leave behind you, *so leave nothing behind*."

"But it's *sand*."

"If you cannot hide where you go on sand, then you do not go on sand." She pointed. "*That* way, there is stone. *That* way, there is dry earth. *That* way, there is short grass."

"The dry earth was level, there was no place to hide. And the grass is where *you* were."

"Things are not always easy. But if you want to be safe, you find a way. If the only place to go is a place where you leave footprints," she crouched and swished her tail behind her, "then you do not leave footprints, and the ones who follow will be sure you did not go there."

Reyna peered at the sand behind her mother. It wasn't just brushed aside, it was practically sculpted. With a simple sweep, she'd wiped away the prints. To any but the most trained eye, there was nothing more than a patch of ground swept about by the wind, the same as the rest of the fields and plains.

"Show me again!" Reyna said.

"First we get your brother. He did the same. Then I show you both, and then we eat."

"So you found him, too?"

"I found him first. His reason was better. Not good, but better."

#

Sorrel held her two young ones close to ward off the cold. Others might have needed a fire to cook their food and keep them warm, but not her little family. They were malthropes, creatures that shared as many features with foxes as they did with humans. A raw meal was no problem at all, and a thick pelt with a few layers of clothes would keep all but the harshest winds and most frigid nights at bay. Such were some of the benefits of their race. Some of the *few* benefits.

She watched her children crunch messily through the scrawny desert hares that served as their evening meal. Her own meal had been a few mice she'd caught during the day, barely morsels, but enough for today. Better that the twins get the larger meal. They were growing like weeds. Wren was a bit taller than Reyna, but if they continued to grow as they had over the last few months, within a year or two they would both be taller than their mother. That was good. They got that from their father. In fact, but for having a shade or two darker fur, Wren was the spitting image of his father. His eyes were uncannily similar, and already he had the beginnings of the wiry-strong build. Reyna took after Sorrel, fur the color of wine and cream and a body built for sneaking. She was clever, too, but with enough curiosity to get her in trouble if she wasn't careful.

Sorrel tugged at the hoods she'd fashioned for them, pulling them up over their pointed ears and smoothing them down. She smiled. That, at least, was one benefit of how quickly they were growing. She was getting plenty of practice with her needle and thread. It was so much easier to steal a bolt of cloth and some thread than to steal clothes that would be small enough that her little ones wouldn't trip over them but not so small they wouldn't outgrow them in a few weeks.

"I can't believe you caught these," Reyna said, her cheeks stuffed with a healthy mouthful.

"Uh-huh. Both of them at the same time!" Wren said proudly. "I could have had three, but I was afraid these two would get away if I went for the third."

"Your brother is a good hunter, but he chooses bad times to hunt," Sorrel said. "He charged right out into the open when he chased these. It is why I caught him so fast."

"It was just the game, Mama," Wren said. "I knew it was *you* that was after me."

Sorrel narrowed her eyes.

"Wren!" Reyna hissed in reprisal.

"Why do we play the game?" Sorrel asked the question with all of the power and solemnity of the beginning of a prayer.

"We play the game so that we will know how to keep away from those who would kill us," the twins replied together.

Sorrel continued. "And who wants to kill us?"

"Everyone, always," they replied.

"And how do we stay alive?"

"By being faster," Wren said.

"And by being smarter," Reyna said.

"Why?"

"Because being faster doesn't help if you don't know where to run," Wren said.

"And being smarter doesn't help if you can't do what needs to be done," Reyna said.

"And for as long as we've played the game, what has happened?"

"You catch us."

"And what does that mean?"

"You're faster and smarter than us."

"And what does *that* mean."

"Someone *else* could be faster and smarter than us."

"And if *they* catch you?"

The twins drew their fingers across their throats. "Dead."

"That's right," Sorrel said, mollified. "Don't you forget that. And Wren, you play properly, or what happens to you isn't my fault, it is yours."

"I know, Mama. Sorry, Mama," Wren said, eyes cast down.

"You caught a meal for you and your sister. That is enough that you should not be sorry. But learn from it. Always learn from it." She leaned low and uttered in a conspiratorial whisper, "And what do we learn at suppertime?"

The twins playfully tried to pull away, knowing what came next, but Sorrel was too quick. She wrapped her arms around them and hugged them tight, tickling their bellies through the layers of earth-tone fabric they wore. They giggled and squirmed.

"Fill a hungry belly and grow up strong," Sorrel said. She released them and tousled their hair under their hoods. "Fill a hungry mind and grow up smart. Do both and you'll live long enough to do the same for *your* young. Now come, in front here."

The Story of Sorrel

Sorrel raked their unruly hair into submission and cleaned their faces with a few quick licks. With the children thus tidied up after supper, she threw her outermost cloak around them and pulled them tight to her. "Today you both lost the game, but Wren lost first, so Reyna chooses the story."

"For once," Wren teased.

Reyna looked sagely into the middle distance, considering the matter carefully.

"If you don't know what to ask for, I do," Wren blurted.

"No! I earned it," Reyna said. "I just want to pick something good."

"This is good. This is a thing you should do. But do it quickly, because we should sleep," Sorrel said.

"Um… Did you play the game when you were little? Or is it just for us?"

"It is not for you. It is for all of us. When I was your size, every day I played the game. And all the time. And though it was the same, it was *not* the same. Because sometimes it was mother or father. But sometimes it was someone else. Sometimes the game was *not* a game. And that is how always you must treat it."

"Why was it sometimes not a game?" Reyna asked. "Why was it sometimes a real hunt?"

"It was not so long ago that we were there. You should remember it."

"The place before the boat?" Wren said.

"Yes. That place. That is what it was like. The place it was so dangerous I did not even let you play the game."

"That's where you grew up?" Reyna said.

"It is and it isn't," Sorrel said. "I grew up someplace different. Someplace colder. But it was much the same. Many men. Many things that are as bad as men. Man-type things. And always wanting to hunt a malthrope."

"But you grew up strong," Reyna said. "You were the fastest and the smartest."

"No, I was not. Always there is someone who is faster. Always there is someone who is stronger. The strongest thing you'll ever see fears something."

"But you never lost the *game*," Wren said.

"Who told you this, that I never lost the game? You would not be here if I did not lose the game. We would not be in this place if I did not lose the game."

Reyna shook her head, hair tumbling into her eyes again. "I don't understand. You said where you came from if you lost the game…" She drew her finger across her throat. "Dead."

"Most times this is true. But sometimes the beings above us, they have other plans."

"So there was someone faster and smarter than you?"

"Smarter than me? No. Not in the ways that matter. But on that day, and only that day, yes, he was faster."

"Oh… *oh*… You're talking about Papa," Reyna said.

"That is right, little kit," she said, nuzzling her young one.

"We *know* that story," Wren said. "That doesn't count as the story."

"I know. I know the story I want," Reyna said. "Why didn't Papa come along?"

"Yeah… Yeah, he was in the boat with us at first. Why didn't he stay?"

Sorrel released a breath through her nose. "Teyn was… I said he was not smart. That is a part of it. But there is more… What are the words?" She shut her eyes and twisted up her face, searching her mind for the proper way to phrase it.

"Why don't you just speak Crich, Mama?" Reyna asked.

"I do not speak Crich because today I speak Tresson. And also you. For practice."

"But you're bad at Tresson," Wren said. "*We* speak Tresson better than you."

"Yes! I know this, because I make sure the way you are speaking is a right way to be speaking." She paused and attempted the sentence more slowly. "Because I make sure you are speaking the right way. It is easier to learn right than learn wrong and change."

"But why do we learn all these languages?" Reyna asked. "There's only ever the two of us. We only ever talk to each other."

"Because that is the way it is today, but tomorrow? Maybe not. What did I say? Feed a hungry mind. So we practice Crich, and we practice Varden, and we practice Tressor language." She shut her eyes tight. "We practice *Tresson*. If I knew how to speak the elf language and the dwarf language, we practice that too. So you, my little ones, are smarter than me. … Now what did I talk about before this?"

"You were saying why Papa didn't come with us."

"Yes, yes. And it was a good reason, I think. Who are we most afraid of? Who do we play the game to be ready for?"

"Man," Wren said.

"And elves," Reyna said.

"And dwarves," Wren added.

"And—" Reyna began.

"Yes, yes. It is all of this. It is all the same. These are the ones we fear. And I said just now that always there is someone smarter and faster and stronger. Someone *they* fear. Teyn… Teyn decided there were things he had to do. Things that if he did not do, no one would. It was important to him. Maybe more important than me, maybe not, but I did not wait for him to decide. I let him go. And then, just before the boat, I lost the game again, and he won. And he was different. Now he was the thing *man* feared. And man *hates* the things man fears. Even more than man hates you or me. Even more than man hates any malthrope. I think… I think maybe it *was* important that he be that thing. Man *deserves* a thing to fear. And to be that thing, he made himself faster. And stronger. … And I think also smarter. Because he knew that what he was, he could not stop being. And that thing would bring dark things with it. He decided it was best that we be safe, and for us to be safe, we could not be with him."

"That's silly. Even if *he* couldn't keep us safe, *you* could," Wren said.

"I am not so sure this is so. Something in him changed… He was… *more*… Always his eyes had pain. I do not know a malthrope with eyes that don't have pain. But when I saw him last… his eyes... he had seen things. He had *done* things. The things that could darken someone as strong as Teyn… if they left their mark on him… if for a moment I thought such a thing might find its way to you through him… no. Many things he did wrong, but this he did right."

Sorrel took a slow breath and pulled her arm from Wren to wipe her eyes. "This is not a story. If you do not want a story, then it is time for sleep."

Wren hissed across to his sister. "Ask for the story about the purple stones."

"If you want your story, you win the game," Sorrel said.

"No, Mama. I like that story too," Reyna said.

The little malthrope tugged a cord around her neck to reveal a palm-size purple stone, polished smooth and wrapped in a carefully woven net to hold it in place. Sorrel cupped her daughter's stone pendant in her hand. As she stared at it, a smile came to her lips, and a dash of pain came to her gaze.

"Always I tell you this story." Sorrel tugged Reyna's shirt out and tucked the stone away. "You know it by heart."

"Please?" they said in unison.

Sorrel sighed. "Very well. Next time, you should pick from me a different story."

She gathered them a little closer. When she spoke again, it was with a sweeping, airy tone. Her twins wriggled closer and shut their eyes to enjoy the scenes the words would paint.

"A long time ago, before my father or mother or their fathers or mothers were born, there was a little malthrope named Swift."

#

If there was ever a malthrope better than all the rest, that was Swift. He could run very fast, but that was not the reason he was called Swift. They called him Swift because he could think very fast, something every good malthrope should learn to do. He lived in a place called the Great Forest. It was a wonderful place, filled with fat deer and foolish hunters. Swift lived his life the way a malthrope should. He stalked and he hunted. He ate and he rested. When danger was near, he hid, and when danger found him, he ran.

One day, Swift was drinking from his favorite place. It was a stream where the water was clear and cool and the elves were far, far away. Only today, something was wrong. Today, the elves were *not* far away. There were many of them, and they were close. Too close. They used evil magics to get near this place, or else the sharp scent and keen hearing of Swift would have let him know they were coming for him.

Let that be a lesson to you. Always there is a way for those who wish to hurt you to find you, so always you must plan for the day that they do, so you will be ready.

He sniffed the air. One by one, he counted the scents that he did not recognize. He counted one, and then two. He counted three, and then four. And finally, he counted five. The fifth, he knew, was the leader. And how did he know? Because the leader is the one who smells least of hard work, and most of easy days. Swift knew it was smart to know where to find the leader. Elves and dwarves and other things like man, they do not know how to be alone, like we do. They listen to what the leaders say. They do what the leaders tell them to do. So it is always best to know where the leader is. Keep him quiet and no one will act. Trick him and you trick all who follow him.

Also, it is always a him. When smelling for a leader, smell for a him. Man-type things think that the males are best because the males are biggest. It is one of the ways that man-type things are fools.

But that is not the story. The story is about Swift and what he did when he smelled the elves come near. What *should* he do? He should run. But they were all around, and elves are a very fast sort of man-type thing. Not as fast as Swift, but fast enough to catch him if he got too near. What should he do instead? He should hide. But he smelled the bad smells of potions and strange smoke. Magic things. When man-type things have magic things, hiding may not do. If Swift was a man-type thing, he might fight. Man-type things love to fight. But that is why you must never fight them. If a thing loves to do something, do not try to do it better. You find the thing they cannot do, and try to do *that* better.

Swift could feel the bad magics. He could hear the cruel talking. He listened from the trees, and he knew that they were after him.

"They say this is the place where Swift makes his home," said the leader elf, who had a name that did not matter.

Swift lowered his head, and he felt foolish. No one should know of a good malthrope. But Swift had many adventures. The adventures I tell you of each night. And adventures take a name and spread it to the winds. Many will hear it, and those many will come. So you must never have an adventure, or you will have a hard time like Swift.

The leader elf kept talking. "Today, we shall catch Swift. We shall sell him and have great wealth."

Many seek to sell a malthrope. Parts of us are worth very much. And the parts that are not? They throw away. It is why some of them hunt us. It is why the leader elf hunted Swift.

"Tell me where to find him. Use your bad magic," the leader elf said to his wizard. "And soldiers be ready. We must keep him alive, so the parts we want do not spoil. And we will sell the pieces, and we will have much money for all of us."

Swift could hear the stretch of bows. He could feel the tingle of magic. He could hear the rustle of nets. The elves would have him if they wanted him. They would have had him already, except that the leader elf was talking. Talking is not fighting. And talking is not hunting. Talking is as good as nothing, so Swift knew if he wanted to stay alive, he needed to keep the leader elf talking. Swift thought and he thought. He thought fast, and he thought long. He thought of all the ways he could run, of all the ways he could fight. He thought of what should come next, and what would come after that. He thought until he had thought of everything that might happen. He thought until he was sure of every step on the path, from trapped in a tree to safe in the woods. Only when he had done all that thinking did he take the first step. Only then did he jump down for all to see.

Jumping down is a foolish thing. But a foolish thing is not foolish if we think long and hard. If we know that the thing is the best thing we can do, then we do the thing, foolish or not. And Swift knew.

"There, we have him! Throw the nets now!" the leader elf cried.

The nets flew. They fell upon Swift. He was fast enough to run, but no malthrope is faster than an arrow, and these elves had them. So he let the nets bind him, because a net is better than an arrow if one has no other choice.

"We have you! You, mally, belong to us!" said the leader elf. "And we will sell you because you are worth a fortune."

Swift lowered his head and he spoke. "Oh leader elf, you who are wise and strong," Swift said.

The leader elf was not wise or strong, of course. If he were strong, he would not have been a leader. The strong do what the leaders say. And if he were wise, he would not have been in the forest. Wise men do not do the things that are hard; they have others do them. But a man-type thing likes to hear nice things, even if they are lies. So Swift said these nice things, and he said more.

"You wish to sell me," Swift said, "because you seek wealth. But if I can offer you more wealth than you would get from me, would you let me go?"

"You are a malthrope. You have no wealth to offer," the leader elf said.

The Story of Sorrel

"That is not so!" Swift said. "I have this!"

And Swift reached into his cape. From inside he pulled a beautiful stone. The color was purple, a very hard color of stone to find. Even when it was dry, it shined like morning dew. He held it up.

"You will not find a finer stone in all of the great woods. It is worth more than I am by far. I will give it to you if you let me go."

"Ha-ha!" the leader elf said. "I have you, and so I have the stone. I do not need to let you go."

"But, leader elf, so wise and so brave, you can have so much more if you let me go. Because I know where there are more stones like this. Five stones more. Let me go and I will fetch them for you."

This was a lie, of course. Swift knew that the stone he held was finer by far than any in the forest. There were no more like it. But like before, a man-type thing will believe a thing if the thing is something he wants to believe. So he believed there was more wealth to be had.

Another day, this would have been enough. They would have let Swift go to fetch the other stones, and Swift would have run and never returned. But today, the leader elf was not as much of a fool as Swift would like.

"If I let you go, you will not come back. Instead, you will lead me to the stones. Soldiers, lock a chain on his neck. Wizards make it so that only by my word can it be opened."

If ever you are in chains, you are in a bad place and you have done many wrong things, but Swift knew this might happen. He had thought this through.

"You are very good and wise, leader elf. I will do as you say. And please, take this first stone to keep."

The leader elf took the stone, and he locked it away. He was very suspicious, which is a good thing to be, but not so suspicious as to keep Swift from seeing where he put the stone. It was in a locked box with other coins and stones, in a tied sack, in the bag on the saddle of the horse. Swift watched it all.

With soldiers holding his chains, Swift marched through the woods. He climbed steep hills. He trudged through painful brambles. The elves were not as strong as Swift and grew tired. They made camp and, while they slept, Swift opened the saddlebag. He untied the sack. He plucked the key from the elf leader and unlocked the box. From inside he took the stone and a handful of coins. One by one, he placed a coin in the pockets of the other sleeping elves, then replaced the box and key.

The next day he made a show of searching. When the time was right, he dropped the stone into the dirt.

"Here, oh wise and brave one. And there are many more like it, and I will lead you to them."

The leader elf was pleased. He placed the stone in his box and demanded Swift continue to lead him to more. For five long days, he led them through the woods. Each night he would take back the stone and more of the coins. Each day he would pretend to find the stone and present it once more.

It was not until the sixth day that the leader elf noticed how empty the box had become.

"What is this?" he said. "I have been robbed. You have done this, you horrible mally!"

Of course the elf leader would think Swift was the thief. All malthropes are thieves to man-type things.

"Oh wise one," Swift said. "I did not! See how I carry no coins. See how I carry no stones."

The elf leader shouted, "Someone has stolen my things. All of you, turn out your pockets."

One by one, the soldiers and wizard emptied their pockets. Gold coins and silver coins spilled to the ground.

"Thieves! Traitors! All of you!" the elf leader cried.

The other elves did not like being called thieves. Man-type things always call others by names they cannot stand to be called. The soldiers raised their weapons. The wizard raised his special stone. All were angry with the leader elf.

"Free me, oh wise one," Swift said quickly. "Only I have not lied to you. If you promise my safety, I shall defend you!"

The elf leader, with no one left to fight his battles for him, quickly spoke the words that would break the chains. Swift was free. And he did not keep his word, because a word to a man-type thing is no word at all. He ran into the forest, and the terrible elves sliced and magicked and beat each other until they were all dead.

#

"And the next day, Swift returned to take the swords, and the gold." She tapped Reyna's pendant. "And the stone. The end."

The twins softly clapped, their faces aglow with smiles.

"I love that one," Reyna said. "Swift is so smart."

"What do we learn from this story?" Sorrel asked. "What lessons does Swift teach us? There are many."

"Elves are stupid and we should lie to them," Wren said.

Sorrel shook her head. "No. That is not the lesson."

Reyna piped up. "Elves can be smart, but they can also be stupid."

"*And* we should lie to them," Wren amended.

"Yes. What else?"

"If you are in chains, you did something wrong, so you have to be extra smart to get out," Reyna said.

"And? More lessons."

"And… you should only do a stupid thing if there are no more smart things to do," Wren said.

"Good, and more. You have heard this story many times. You should know all of the lessons."

Reyna scratched her head. "Oh! Stealing is always a good thing to do."

Sorrel crossed her arms. "Who tells you that stealing is a good thing to do? Swift did not steal anything in the story."

"Right, because he only took the stone, which was his already," Wren said. "And the coins, but he gave them back."

"But what about the swords and things, after they were all dead?" Reyna said.

"You can't steal from a dead person. Everyone knows that," Wren mocked.

"This is true, but also it is not," Sorrel said. "Listen close, because this is very important. It is two pieces. First, you should never take anything unless it belongs to you. Second, anything that someone else cannot stop you from getting belongs to you. Swift takes an elf's gold, that is the elf's fault for not keeping it, not Swift's fault for taking it."

"Oh… right. Because if I find an apple on a tree, I'm not stealing from the tree," Wren said.

"Taking things from people is just… harvesting," Reyna reasoned.

"Yes! Now one last lesson and we all get some sleep."

"Adventures are bad," Reyna and Wren said in unison.

"That's right. Now sleep for you both."

Chapter 2

Just as the sun began to paint the sky, Sorrel roused the twins for a new day of lessons.

"Up. Up. Both of you. The prey will soon be stirring, and you must be ready," she said, pulling free her cloak to let the lingering cold help wake the sleepy children.

"But, Mama..." murmured Reyna, pulling her own cloak tighter around her.

Wren was a bit more enthusiastic at the prospect of a hunt.

"Can we try for a deer today, Mama?" Wren said. "I almost got one last time."

"We are in the desert, Wren. This is not a place for deer. There won't be prey so large here. In the forest, and in the plains, there you can find big prey. In the farms of man and the things like man as well. But not here."

"Aw… Why did we leave the forest then, Mama?" Wren said.

"Because the things like man like the forest, and so we must not be there. We are better hunters. We can live anywhere. And to be safe, we must live where others cannot."

"But won't that be hard?"

"The good things to do, the right things, they are not the easy things. But now is not for talking. Now is for hunting. Reyna, you listen, and you follow. Hunt as well as Wren today. And Wren, hide as well as Reyna. You each must do both."

"Yes, Mama," they said in unison.

The twins stood and raised their noses for a long, slow sniff.

"Uh-uh-uh," Sorrel lightly scolded. "What do we use first? Before even our noses?"

"Our heads?" Reyna said.

"This is so. Where is it that we should start our hunt?"

Reyna and Wren mused quietly.

"Oh, near the water!" Wren said.

Sorrel tousled his hair. "Good, yes. You have a good head. Always by the water. Come."

They turned to the east. Sorrel always made certain to spend the night near enough to water to reach it quickly, but far enough to avoid providing a warning to any of the animals who might venture near for a morning drink. In an arid plain like this, remaining hidden meant moving much farther from the water than she would have liked. Without even tall grass to crouch in, they were at the mercy of the low rolling hills to provide their cover. It wasn't ideal, but little in their lives was.

The family crept low to the ground, eyes steady, ears perked, noses sampling the air. Sorrel closed her eyes and focused on the way the wind ruffled her whiskers. There was barely a breeze. That was good. Their scent would not travel. Still, with no cover and a great deal of distance between themselves and the meager collection of rabbits and lizards near the water, they would need to move with painful slowness, and even that might not be enough.

Sorrel silently signaled the twins to drop into a shallow gully out of sight of the water. When they were hidden, she motioned for them to watch closely and gathered up the powdery soil in handfuls, patting it into her fur and clothing with an artist's precision. Soon she was covered from head to toe, a layer of dust perfectly blending her color to that of the land. The twins imitated, not as skillfully, but Sorrel finished the job for them and they resumed the hunt.

A long stalk and a frenzied sprint later, Sorrel snatched up a pair rabbits. Reyna caught a lizard, and Wren caught a rabbit of his own. It was a fine hunt, and left them with full bellies and the rest of the day to digest, learn, and plan.

#

During the day, when they did not have to worry about finding prey, they moved with a bit less care. They were still mindful of those who might hunt them, but Sorrel neither saw nor smelled anything that concerned her. The desert stretched out to the north, and the thinning remnants of the plains and forest stretched out to the south. There was little to obscure her view. Breezes and gusts, when they came, carried scents from miles around. It was as safe as she was ever likely to feel while out in the open. Her children knew her well enough to know that if she was not concerned and cautious, they need not be either. It seldom took long for the questions to begin to flow.

"Mama?" Reyna said. "We are going north."

"Yes."

"There's just more desert to the north."

"Yes, Reyna."

"Why do we keep going? The desert is bad!"

"But how bad?"

"Who cares? It is bad!"

"We need to know. Know always how bad it is. Know how far you can go. Because if someone follows, you need to know how far you can go, and for how long."

"But no one is following us, Mama," Wren said.

"That is why we go now. Now if we make a mistake, if we go too far, we can come back. If someone follows and we make a mistake, we don't come back. But if we know, then when we go, *they* go too far. And *they* don't come back."

Wren slumped a bit. "So we have to keep looking and listening and sniffing."

"We always do. Always."

"Always forever?" Reyna asked.

"You should not ask questions you know the answer to."

Reyna's shoulders slumped too. "Sorry, Mama."

They walked in silence, but for the children, the silence was heavier. Sorrel looked down to them.

"Also you should not stay silent when you have something you need to say."

Reyna looked at her feet and huffed. "Is there ever going to be a place where we don't have to do this? Where we can just *be* instead of always worrying?"

Sorrel looked to the north. "I do not know. But I think there is a place like that. I have not found it. But always I am looking for it. That is why there is the game. The game keeps us alive until we find a place like that. The game teaches us to know when we have *found* a place like that. That is why you must be good at the game. Because maybe I will not be with you when you find the place. Maybe you will need to know for yourself."

"The game is for so many reasons…" Wren said.

"The game is everything," Sorrel said.

Wren sniffed the air and glanced about. "Can we start early today, then?"

Reyna nodded. "Yes! Can we? I know *just* which way to go."

Sorrel grinned. "Now is a good time to start."

She shut her eyes and crouched down. When they were certain she could not see, they scampered away. The soft crunch of sand was barely audible beneath their feet. She breathed in their scent until it began to fade. They chose their direction well. It didn't take long before the wind was wafting their scent away rather than blowing it toward her. In minutes, none of her senses spoke of them beyond the lingering scent of their trail. It was the one thing that no amount of care or wisdom could entirely eliminate, and thus it was the reason she knew that she would be able to find her children no matter how carefully they played the game. They simply couldn't move quickly enough for their trails to be cold before she could find them. But they didn't need to know that. The harder they worked at an impossible goal, the closer they came to doing the impossible. And doing the impossible was very nearly what it would take to live to a ripe old age as a malthrope.

She opened her eyes and scanned the ground. Little footprints traced swift paths away, each vanishing as they found parallel paths along ground that wouldn't show their passage.

"They walk together…" Sorrel mused. "Maybe good, maybe bad. We will see how far they get."

#

"Hurry up, Reyna," Wren called, his voice almost silent but still quite loud enough for his sister's sensitive ears.

"Not so fast," she objected, rushing along after him.

Both were running at a crouch, but Wren was managing much longer strides.

"If we go fast, we get farther. If we get farther, she takes longer to find us. Far enough, fast enough, and we win the game!" Wren said.

"But I can't keep up. And we don't know where we're going!"

"So? I never know where I'm going. I just go the ways I *can*. Right now we don't have to worry about where to, we just have to worry about away *from*. And we're going away from Mama."

Wren skidded to a stop as the winding valley between two sandy hills abruptly ended, denying them cover.

"*See,*" Reyna huffed, catching up to him and trying to recover. "It isn't always about being faster. We can also *hide*."

"We can't hide so close to where we started, Mama will find us before the sun even gets close to the horizon. And then *neither* of us gets a story."

"Not if we hide really good," Reyna said.

The Story of Sorrel

Wren wrinkled his nose and sniffed the air. He couldn't smell his mother, but that didn't mean much. For all he knew, she was right on top of them. Retracing their steps would cost them some of the precious distance they'd gotten as part of their head start. But they *had* chosen their path poorly. Good cover from this point forward would be hard to find.

"Fine," Wren said. "You're a better hider than me. Where would *you* hide?"

They'd been following some firm ground that didn't show prints, probably the dried-up bed of a river. The sand that spread outward and upward along the dunes was much looser. It would easily show their prints if they tried to travel across it. She pawed at the sandy ground with her fingers. The top layer of the soil was dry, but not far below the surface was moist sand that stuck to her fur. She started to dig.

"First, we use the sand, we make ourselves harder to see," Reyna said. "Like with Mama earlier. Only with the sand here, so we match."

She patted handfuls of the sticky sand against her outfit. Wren did the same.

"Mama sees very good," Wren said. "It won't be enough."

"But it won't be nothing."

"What do we do after the sand?"

"Um…" Reyna said, her uncertainty more than evident.

"You don't know, do you?" Wren said, grinning smugly as he smeared some sand on his face.

"*You* should have ideas *too*. That's why I wanted to run *together*. Mama says we need to be fast *and* strong *and* smart. I'm fast and smart, and you're fast and strong. We have to be together to be all three."

"I'm smart too!" Wren said, realizing what his sister perceived to be his shortcoming. "I'll show you."

He stared at the ground, now churned up by their digging. "First we need to fix this. She'll know what we did if we don't."

"*I know that.*" Reyna started smoothing the sand over. "That's not the idea we need."

Wren helped her pat and smooth away the evidence of their digging. "This ground… this ground is very much like the ground we find rabbits near."

"No hunting, Wren. That's what got you caught last time."

"No, no! The rabbits like to dig and hide in holes. If they get inside deep enough, I can't get them. Maybe we can do that!"

"We don't have time to dig a hole."

"Maybe we can *find* a nice big hole. Or a little one that we can make big fast. Look, there is more sand like that this way, and all along that part there. And Mama is probably back the other way, since we can't smell her, and that means she's downwind. So we go that way, we look for holes, and we hide in them."

Reyna nodded. "Yes. That is a good idea. If you can't be like the hunter, be like the hardest-to-get prey. Mama says that all the time!"

They hurried off, rarely standing taller than a crawl. The sand did a wonderful job of hiding them, making fur and clothes alike the same tawny color of the soil. It even masked their scent a bit. The layer of musty earthiness over their own scent wouldn't fool Sorrel for more than a moment, but that was a moment longer than not at all.

As the pair dashed, they set their minds wholly upon two simple things: getting as far away as they could, and finding a good place to dig. So excited and enthusiastic were they about their new plan that they began to forget about other important lessons they had learned.

#

Sorrel followed the scent and path of her twins.

"They are trying new things…" she mused to herself, noticing a half-hidden paw print. "I will stay back. Let them know that new things like this are sometimes good…"

She moved after them with far greater care than she would ever take while hunting food. For the little ones, playing the game correctly was the relatively simple matter of remaining hidden until the sun set. For that, Sorrel had to stay far enough away that they could not detect her, but near enough that she never truly lost them. Caring for her young was an endless balancing act, making them always aware of the dangers of the world and teaching them to face those dangers, but never allowing them to face those dangers alone until she knew they were ready.

She came to the end of the riverbed they had been following. They'd covered their tracks well, though in this case it didn't help much. She knew they'd come this way, and as she hadn't seen them scamper over the dunes, they could only have fled along the valley between them. Sorrel traced the path forward with her eyes. A few twists, a few turns, but with the way the wind was blowing and where the sun was in the sky, Reyna and Wren could only safely choose a single route from here without risking being seen.

Sorrel nodded. They'd cornered themselves. It was an understandable mistake, and one that she would have made herself at their age, but it was a serious enough one that she couldn't allow them a win today. If a hunter of her skill had truly sought them as prey, they were as good as caught. She would give them a few hours more to see if they realized their mistake. Perhaps she could afford to linger long enough for them to earn another story. This little adventure reminded her of a fine one...

She heard a quiet buzz. Her ear flicked. Near the water, the air was thick with insects. Small, annoying bugs drifted in the breeze. Large, swooping ones made meals of them. This was certainly the thrumming beat of a large insect. But she was far from the water. There were no small insects around. She held perfectly still and waited. The buzzing came and went. She watched with her peripheral vision, waiting for the source of the sound to come into view. It stubbornly refused to. She narrowed her eyes and released a soft sigh. Sorrel had never known a dragonfly to be clever enough to stay out of sight. That left just one possibility.

Her ears pivoted to follow its sound. Timing would be important. This was the sort of thing she wouldn't get a second chance at. For Sorrel, that was true of most things. She was quite accustomed to making the moment count. The soft flutter of wings drew near. Nearer. Nearer still. At the precise instant it was near enough, she swiped her hand blindly through the air. Her aim was true. A tiny form slapped into the palm of her hand.

Sorrel raised a small, struggling creature to her face. It was barely larger than the palm of her hand: a fairy. She'd had little experience with them, but her rare encounters had never been with a specimen like this. As far as she could tell, it was a male. He had dark, almost copper-colored skin. Black hair formed a frazzled nest atop his head. She knew better than to loosen her grip to inspect his body, but it felt as though he wore little in the way of clothes.

"There is no water near. No fire, either. An earth fairy, then? Does such a thing exist, I wonder?" Sorrel murmured to herself.

The fairy struggled and trilled. It was deceivingly strong, but not strong enough to pull itself free of her grip. Sorrel pulled it close to her face.

"You should not be so curious, fairy," she said quietly. "Now I let you go, and you leave me be. Or maybe I use these on you next time."

She peeled her lips in a snarl. When she was sure he'd gotten a good look at what he'd be facing if he continued to bother her, she let the little thing go. It buzzed upward and she turned back to the breeze to sample for the scent of her brood. She shut her eyes and took a long, deep whiff. The air carried the scent of sand, dry grass... but not Reyna and Wren.

Sorrel took another breath, slower and longer this time. The trail her children had taken was right below her nose. She should smell it. There was no way she could have lost the scent. She dropped down, sniffing again and again. Not until her nose was buried in the soil did she get so much as a hint of the scent she was after.

She cocked her head, then glanced over her shoulder. The fairy was well out of her reach, but still near enough for her to see the flutter of his wings and hear their buzz.

"That thing... is it... changing the wind?" she mused.

Her chest tightened. A flash of anxiety burned in her stomach. She craned her neck slightly and scanned her surroundings. The sand around her had shifted. The short grass all bent in the same direction, waving softly away from her. Her eyes settled on a tawny bit of landscape. It seemed perfectly innocuous. But something about it, something about the shadows and the sweep of it, sparked something in her mind.

"I don't like this... We will not play the game today. Someone *else* is playing the game."

She stood and put her fingers to her lips, readying a piercing whistle to summon the twins. Before she could, the confounding wind kicked up. Sand scoured her face and blasted her eyes. She stumbled back, eyes tearing and blinking away the grit. Rising wind whistled in her ears, but it couldn't fully mask the sound of footsteps charging toward her.

Sorrel sprang blindly back and away from the hill's peak. She desperately wanted to rush to her children, to sweep them up and keep them safe. But now was not the time. To run to them now would only lead these attackers, whoever the were, right toward them.

Her mind and heart raced as she bounded blindly down the slope. Everywhere she turned, the wind followed, spraying in her eyes. The air was thick with dust and debris. Each heaving breath choked her lungs with sand. Hidden among the wail of the wind was the half-heard whistle of rope whipping through the air. She turned her bounding run into a wild leap, but something coiled tight about her leg. She thumped to the ground, and in a heartbeat, a dozen hands pinned her to it. She was caught. And she'd never even seen the faces of those who had bested her.

Chapter 3

The sun slid ever lower. Reyna and Wren huddled in the shadows of a burrow they'd hastily dug. It had taken time and effort to claw out a space large enough for the two of them. Then came something that was more of an art, the sculpting and scattering of the sand to hide that they'd ever been there at all.

Hours crept by. They were smeared with fresh soil, a thick layer patted into their fur. If not for the glitter of their squinted eyes, one could almost imagine there was nothing but a pair of wind-blown motes of sand where the twins were hiding.

It wasn't a comfortable place to hide, but they were used to that. Safety and comfort weren't the same thing, and of the two, safety was better. They were hungry and thirsty, too. But food and water could wait. The sun was quite near the horizon, and they were so very close to winning the game.

The twins started to wriggle and fidget as the final sliver of sun inched down along the horizon. Just a few seconds more. The air didn't carry even a hint of their mother, but that didn't mean a thing. She always seemed to turn up whether they could smell her or not. Finally, the moment came and went. Evening turned to night. They had hidden for the whole of the day.

They had won.

Wren scrambled from the cave and leaped and pranced triumphantly.

"We did it!" he crowed.

"I can't believe it!" Reyna said.

She slipped out and the two joined paws and bounced about. It was a peculiar sight, the pair of malthropes reveling in their victory. Even as the thrill of their first real win seized them, they kept their motions below the peaks of the hills. Even as they cheered and celebrated, they kept their voices barely above a whisper. The pair had mastered the art of stealthy exuberance.

"What do we do now?" Wren asked, a smile still lighting up his face. "What do we win? And how do we tell Mama?"

"I don't know. We must have hidden better than we thought. I would have thought the moment we poked a nose out of the burrow, she would have seen us. Should we call her?" Reyna said.

"You call her."

She crossed her arms. "You have the louder voice."

"I get *scolded* for having the louder voice."

"She can't scold you *now*. We won the game! This is time for a reward!"

"If you aren't afraid of getting scolded, then why don't *you* call for her?"

"Because *you* have the louder *voice*."

Wren glared at her. "Fine. But if she yells at me, I'm telling her you told me to do it." He took a deep breath and called out, "Mama!"

In truth, the call was barely above speaking volume, but after hours of being too cautious to breathe too loudly, it was downright startling. They dropped down against the slope of the hill, ears twisting this way, eyes peering that way. Sorrel did not come.

"*Mama!*" Wren called, now a genuine shout.

"Why won't she come…" Reyna said with a chill.

"I don't know. She can't be far. She's never far."

"You don't think… something happened to her, do you?"

He tipped his head up and stated in a very matter-of-fact manner. "Nothing happened to Mama, because nothing happened to *us*. Mama's better at hiding and running than we are, so if something was going to happen to anyone, it would happen to *us* and *she'd* get away."

"Then where *is* she?"

Wren turned the possibilities over in his head. "We never won the game before, right?" he said.

"Right."

"So we don't *really* know what happens next in the game. Maybe there's a second part."

"But why wouldn't she tell us that part?"

"Maybe that's *part* of the part. Maybe we have to figure it out on our own," Wren suggested.

"So what do we do, then?"

"I don't know. You're better at figuring."

"I don't want to figure. I want Mama," she said, shrinking down below the sandy peak.

"The sooner we figure out what she wants us to figure out, the sooner we get her back. And a reward!"

"What do you think it'll be?" Reyna asked, her fear tempered by the promise of a prize.

"Um… Remember when we were by that bazaar down south? She stole those sweets?"

Reyna held up a finger. "Uh-uh-uh. She *found* those sweets in a shop. Remember? If they can't keep them away from us, they don't belong to them."

"Right, right. But remember how good they were? I bet she kept some. I bet she has a sweet for each of us."

"You think?" Reyna said eagerly.

"Mama *always* keeps some of something important. And if sweets are the reward for winning the game, they're very important. So get to figuring!" He shut his eyes and hunkered down, lips curled in pleasant memory. "I hope it's the chewy one…"

Reyna rolled over to place her back on the cooling sand of the hill. "What would be the next part of the game…" she murmured. "The game is all about hunting."

"No," Wren corrected. "It's all about running and hiding."

"They're the same thing, Wren," she countered. "We're running and hiding. *She's* hunting."

He tipped his head back and forth. "I *guess*. But *mostly* it's running and hiding."

She tugged at the edge of her shawl. "So if it's about running and hiding *and* hunting… we didn't do any hunting yet."

"Hunting is a different game. She teaches that separate."

"Maybe she doesn't. Maybe it's all one big game. Remember? On the safe days? She lets you and me play tag."

"And I always win because *you* don't run as fast as me."

"Except when I hide."

"That's not tag, that's hide and seek."

"You can still hide during tag, Wren. And that's not what I'm talking about. When we play tag, if you tag me, then it's my turn to tag you."

"Yeah, so?"

"So we finished the hiding part. Maybe the next part of the game is the *hunting* part and Mama hides."

"You think?" Wren said.

She shrugged. "It could be. Maybe that's why she doesn't answer. Because she's hiding now."

"But that's not fair! Mama's good at hiding. Better than us."

"But she isn't anymore, right? She couldn't find us, so that means we're *as* good at hiding as her. The next part is hunting."

Wren grumbled. "You might be right." He cautiously craned his neck. "Hunting at night is harder, though."

"The next part of the game *would* be harder, wouldn't it?"

She crawled up to peer with him. It was astounding how a little bit of light and a little bit of thought could completely change the way the world looked. All through the day, the field had looked so small. It had seemed like there was nowhere to hide, and no way to get far enough away to have a chance to escape if Sorrel spotted them. Now the field was nothing but nooks and crannies. Every shadow was a yawning abyss that could easily conceal their mother. And everything was so spread out. It would take them ages to reach the best hiding places, all the while scurrying where Sorrel could easily spot them.

"I think you figured right," Wren said. "But I wish you hadn't." He shuddered a bit.

"What's wrong?"

"How do we know when we win? How do we know when *she* wins?"

"We won by sunset. She must win by sunrise, right?"

"A whole night without Mama…" he said. "That's too long."

"The sooner we go, the sooner we find her," Reyna said.

He huffed and nodded. As if it were choreographed, they each raised their nose and took a long sniff, then lowered it for three sniffs along the ground. When they had the scent of the land in their noses, they wordlessly slipped over the hill and into the night.

#

When two creatures have lived every minute by each other's side, learning the same lessons and pursuing the same goals, words cease to be necessary. Both Reyna and Wren knew just how to track a scent and follow a path. It wasn't a matter of one knowing better than the other. It was a matter of one looking left while the other looked right. When two were of one mind, a simple twitch of an eyebrow or flick of an ear could convey volumes of information.

Wren pawed softly at some soil. Reyna watched and knew—this was a footprint that Sorrel had swept away. That meant they were heading in the right direction. Reyna dropped down to sniff the ground. The merest shift of her weight told Wren that she'd found a trace of their mother and they should continue to the east.

It took a few hours, but they were able to find something resembling a trail left by Sorrel. They'd had to circle all the way back to a path they knew they'd followed, so it felt like cheating. Fortunately, if there was one lesson the many adventures of Swift had taught them, it was that it isn't cheating if it's the only way you can win.

Night had fallen. What little light there was came from a crescent moon that was low in the sky. It was plenty for their sharp eyes. Wren and Reyna almost felt confident that they would stumble upon their mother any moment when, quite suddenly, the trail came to an end.

"I don't understand it," Wren said, nose low to the ground. "Even Mama can't just *decide* not to leave a trail."

"Maybe she can. Maybe there's more to learn than we thought," Reyna said.

"But there's no footprints, and nothing like what she leaves behind when she wipes them away."

Reyna crouched and hugged her knees, eyes on the ground. "I've never seen ground look like this before," she said, a chill in her tone.

Wren stood and paced back. The ground *was* in a curious state. The sand was terribly churned up, but the disturbance was a near-perfect circle.

"I don't think she did this…" Reyna murmured.

"She must have done this. Who else could have done this? Mama is just showing us she has more good tricks. Maybe *that's* the reward. We get to learn the better tricks now."

She shook her head. "I don't know. I don't like it."

Wren trotted over and placed a paw on her shoulder. "You look scared."

"I *am* scared."

He waggled a finger at her. "What does Mama say? Don't look scared. If you look scared, the scary people know they are winning."

"Then there *are* scary people," she said.

"No! I didn't say that." He gathered himself up, trying to stand tall and brave. "I'll show you. What does Mama say to do when you are expecting prey and you don't find it?"

"She says look for other hunters."

"That's right. So we look for other hunters, and when we don't find any, that means this is all still the game and we keep looking."

Reyna nodded and let herself tip forward onto all fours. Wren did the same, and they put their noses to work once more. On their way there, they had been scouring every whiff for the very specific, very familiar scent of their mother. It had a way of blinding one to other things. Now they were looking for anything that *wasn't* their mother. That was a very wide net to cast. Each breath that had once registered itself in their mind as nothing at all was now a bouquet of aromas. A dusty old desert rabbit from three days ago. A jackal from a few hours ago. The dry sting of desert shrubs. … And something else.

Wren was the first to notice it, but Reyna caught a whiff a few moments later. Both froze in place. They shut their eyes and held still, as though it took all of their mind and body to make sense of the odor. They lowered their heads and took in a long, thoughtful breath. When they opened their eyes, they locked each other in a disbelieving gaze.

"It can't be," Reyna said.

"What else *could* it be? It isn't my smell, it isn't yours, and it isn't Mama's. But it is *our* smell. It's a malthrope smell." He sniffed again. "Not just one either… Three. There were three malthropes here."

"But there aren't any malthropes but us and Papa! And this isn't Papa's smell."

"We don't *know* there aren't any. Mama knew some back where she came from. There could be more."

The wind shifted. Even without a sniff, both twins dropped to the ground and turned to the southeast.

"More… and they smell the same! Different, but the same!" Wren said, eyes sweeping in the direction of the breeze.

"I don't like it," Reyna said. "Why didn't we smell these things before? We've been through here before. And where's Mama?"

"There!" Wren said.

He sprang to his feet, standing tall as he saw something sprinting toward them in the soft moonlight. The motions were so sure, so swift. The way they hugged the contours of the ground, using paws as well as feet to scramble as quickly and purposefully as they could. It was precisely the way their mother moved. Wren had all but waved and shouted for what he believed to be their mother when a second figure emerged from between two dunes. It moved just as the first had.

"That's not Mama. Not either of them," Reyna said.

"But they're malthropes! They're malthropes like us!" Wren said. "Come on! They *must* know where Mama is."

He took a step toward them, but Reyna caught his arm and held him back.

"What are you doing?" Wren asked. "Malthropes! After all this time, there are more malthropes!"

"We should go. We don't know if they're friendly."

"But they're *malthropes*!"

"Mama said everyone's unfriendly except for us."

"But they *are* us!"

Reyna held tight to his wrist. She looked like her mind was stretched tight between the hope of others like her and the carefully taught fear of outsiders that Sorrel had instilled. Wren glanced back and forth between her and the rapidly approaching malthropes. The fear was real, and deep. And something in the way the others moved toward them seemed wrong. There was no doubt the twins had been seen, and seen for what they were, but there was not joy and charity in the postures of these creatures. They moved with the speed and focus of Sorrel when she was on the tail of a plump meal.

"We'll go... Yeah... We'll go," Wren said.

They turned and launched into a full sprint. A dash of relief and familiarity washed over them. Running, hiding. That, at least, they knew. That, at least, they were good at. But the relief was all too brief. As they bounded north and west, the dim light of the moon offered the briefest glimpse of motion. They had time enough to turn and yelp in fright before a blur of motion and the grip of fingers pulled them both into a well-hidden hole.

The pair struggled and squealed, but whoever had snatched them managed to keep them off balance and moving, half dragging and half leading the frightened little creatures through utter darkness. In just a few strides, even the twins' sharp eyes couldn't see their snouts in front of their faces. They wouldn't know where to run even if they were free. For better or worse, they could only go where they were ushered, deeper and deeper into the cool, dark tunnels.

Chapter 4

The confused, terrified sprint continued in the darkness. Though they didn't stop running for a moment, something in the way these unseen helpers moved was less hostile, less predatory than the malthropes that had been charging their way. When the waves of panic started to calm, Wren and Reyna realized that these, too, smelled like more of the same. Malthropes for sure, though not quite like them.

In time, they stumbled out into the light again, quite far from where they had slipped beneath the dunes. The moon gave them their first clear glimpse of the three creatures that could be either captors or rescuers. Indeed, they were malthropes, but nothing like what the twins had come to expect. They were small, a match for the size of the children. They dressed in rough clothes. Slender, spindly limbs moved them with precision as they vaulted a dried riverbed and vanished into another tunnel. Their fur was the same shades as the sand, creamy yellow, tawny brown, and platinum white. Their snouts were shorter than Reyna's or Wren's. And despite their size, there was something in their movement, in their scent, that made it clear they were adults. A ragged-looking fairy buzzed among them.

The twins looked to one another. Fear had faded to fascination, and even anticipation. If these creatures had ill will, they'd had ample time to show it. And it felt better to be running *with* someone than to be running *from* someone. Without words, Wren and Reyna agreed that they would go where these creatures led. Until they saw whatever they were being taken to, they would not try to escape.

It wasn't until more than an hour of near-constant running later that their strange companions finally slowed. They trotted for a short distance, then came to a stop in what, at first glance, seemed to be little more than a hilly stretch of the arid plain. The fairy regarded the three malthropes for a moment. After a gesture from them, it flitted off over the dunes.

The three mysterious little malthropes stopped their sprint and turned to the children. One by one, they unfolded their ears from the backward, tucked-away twist of their sprint.

Reyna blinked and stared. Wren nearly snickered. The ears were *enormous*. Each creature's ears were nearly as large as the rest of its head. As Reyna gazed in wonder at the odd sight, the three malthropes stared back, silently measuring and judging what they saw. Wren looked around.

The group that had dragged them here comprised a female and two males. One of the males tugged a large bottle from his back and took a long drink of water from within. One by one, the others slaked their thirst, then the bottle was passed to Reyna. She gratefully accepted.

"Is this… oh, wow," Wren said in a hush. "I think this is a town!"

Reyna finished her drink and reluctantly took her eyes from their companions' to look around. While Wren took his turn at the bottle, she discovered what he had. It was subtle, but here and there a sandy mat of woven reeds formed what *could* be a door. If one did not know where to look, one could easily have missed the place, but now that they had a moment, they could see at least a dozen such makeshift doors.

One of the light-furred malthropes chattered something odd and complex. It was the female. She reached forward and turned Reyna to face her once more. She leaned closer, and Reyna felt a stir of concern. Something in the expression seemed less friendly now. The little creature sniffed at her, then glanced down at her own fingers. She pinched and rubbed away the layer of soil she'd wiped from Reyna when she turned her.

One of the males grabbed Wren by the arm and pulled him close. Though he was the same size as Wren, the desert malthrope was quite strong. He tugged at Wren's ear.

"Hey! Stop that!" Wren shouted, shoving him away.

The desert malthrope snatched the bottle out of his paws and splashed it in Wren's face.

"What are you doing?" he sputtered, wiping his eyes.

The water dripped muddily from his face, revealing the red fur that he had so carefully layered with soil while they were hiding.

The three little malthropes chattered angrily to each other. The female pulled a short sword fashioned from a red-green metal. The others revealed dirks tipped with spikes of the same mottled material.

Wren and Reyna leaped back and instantly bounded to a full sprint to escape those who were now certainly their captors. Alas, while they had been trying to make sense of the three strange little malthropes before them, a dozen more had emerged from the hidden entryways of the burrows that made up the town. All were armed with weapons of various sorts. All were the same child-sized, tawny-furred malthropes, and all had the fierce look of someone more than willing to skewer two children rather than let them get away.

Wren bared his teeth and spread his fingers. Reyna clutched his arm.

"Don't…" she breathed through her terror.

"I h-have to protect you. M-mama would want it—"

"Mama says don't fight if you can run, and only fight if you can win," Reyna said, huddling close. "Mama says if you fight, people fight back."

"Th-then what do we do?" he said, crouching down and pulling closer to her.

The other malthropes closed in. Those nearest stowed their weapons and revealed nets and ropes.

"They're going to trap us!" Wren said, swiping at the first of the desert creatures to approach.

"We're already trapped," Reyna said. "And tied up is better than dead."

One of the little malthropes held out a loop of rope. She was chattering insistently. Those flanking her brandished their weapons more vigorously.

"I don't understand!" Wren said, flinching at the gleaming blades.

They chattered more, patience waning.

"We don't understand you!" Reyna said, this time trying Varden rather than Tresson.

Confused glances rippled among the strange little malthropes, but soon their agitation returned.

"Just tell us what you want us to do!" Reyna made the desperate request in the last language she knew, Crich.

At the outburst, the whole of the village seemed to twist their heads and flick their ears at once. A murmur swept across the gathered creatures. Here and there, a single phrase the twins could understand was mixed in.

"*Dragon talk,*" the rope-wielder said.

"What?" Reyna said. "What dragons? Where?"

The malthrope with the rope motioned for them to hold still, then shouted something. The crowd of creatures rippled a bit and parted as a hunched, wizened malthrope, more gray than tan, hobbled up to them.

"Do you understand my words?" he said.

The Elder malthrope spoke with excessive care, as though it was a phrase he was repeating by rote rather than a proper question. Reyna and Wren nodded.

"W-we understand," Reyna said.

"Give your paws to Tessi. She will tie you. You will be safe," he said.

"I don't trust him," Wren rumbled in Tresson again, so that the others could not understand.

"What else can we do?" Reyna said.

Wren clenched his teeth, but offered his hands. The malthrope with the rope, presumably Tessi, cinched the loop tight around his wrists and fashioned a second one for Reyna.

"Swift would have figured a way out of this," Wren moped as he and his sister were led forward.

#

The twins huddled down and waited as the malthropes around them chattered back and forth in their odd little language. Both Reyna and Wren had their paws very firmly tied, and each had a guard assigned. Wren was tense and coiled, ready to spring in the direction of freedom if an opening came, but with each passing moment such an opening seemed less likely. There was something in the gaze of the other malthropes. They watched with the same knowing, predatory gaze their mother had when they caught a glimpse of her during the game. Every motion seemed anticipated. Wren had the very real feeling that if he made a wrong move, not only would his guard know precisely what the young malthrope had in mind, but he would also be fiercely and firmly punished for it.

And yet, despite the dire circumstances, the twins couldn't help but feel wonder at having discovered more of their kind.

"What do you think they are?" Reyna said, looking her own guard over with a bit of fascination mixed in with the fear.

"They're mean malthropes is what they are," Wren said, trying to match the intensity of his captor's gaze. "They aren't even malthropes. They're *mallies*."

Reyna kicked him. "That's a bad word, Wren."

"It's the *right* word. The first malthropes we meet since Papa and they point weapons at us and tie us up. That's not right."

"Still. We don't use the bad words," she said.

A quiet conversation between two of the other villagers came to an end. One of them, a male with a somewhat more elaborate outfit than the others, stepped forward. While most of these desert malthropes wore airy layers of rough, billowy cloth, this one wore clothes cut closer, more tailored. He wore a tunic and trousers. A wide-brimmed hat shaded his face. It had holes for his enormous ears to poke through, and every bit of the outfit was festooned with silver and gold ornaments. He was certainly some manner of chieftain.

"Why did you come here?" he asked.

The question had the same stilted delivery as the Elder's, but the words weren't as precisely formed. There was a residue of the chattery language he'd been speaking earlier.

"You *brought* us here," Wren barked, switching to Crich so he would be understood.

"Why do you disguise yourselves?" he said, reaching out to scratch some of the sandy muck still clinging to Reyna's muzzle.

Wren snapped at him, his jaws narrowly missing the chieftain's fingers. The chieftain laughed and motioned to one of the guards. A lightning motion clamped Wren's jaws in a strong grip. A second guard produced and affixed a muzzle to keep the jaws clamped tight.

The chieftain looked to Reyna. "He bites. Do you bite? Or will you talk?"

She shrank away from him a bit. "I'll talk," she said.

"Why did you disguise yourself?"

"We didn't. We were hiding. We covered ourselves so we could hide in the sand."

"You did not hide from us well enough."

"We weren't hiding from you," Reyna said. "We were hiding from Mama."

The chieftain tipped his head. "You hide from your mother?"

"It's the game. Don't you play the game?"

"Game," he repeated, as though he was completely unfamiliar with the word. "This does not matter. You are forest malthropes. You are Reds. You know you can't come here."

"We didn't even know where here was!"

"The Fennecs and the Reds have been here for generations. We know the lines. We do not *cross* the lines unless we mean to make war." He jabbed a finger at her shoulder. "You disguise yourself. You come to our place. You mean to make war. People who make war become prisoners. But never have there been whelps who make war."

"We *aren't* making war! We come from across the ocean."

"Across the ocean." The chieftain mined through his memories until the words found meanings. "In boats. You come from the place of death."

"Mama just called it Tressor. Except the part north of Tressor. She called it a bunch of names. But I don't remember them. Mama says we don't need to know about that place, because we aren't ever going back there."

"The place across the ocean is not a place that people *come* from. It is a place of death. Malthropes who went there never returned."

"Yeah. It was a bad place. Lots of people who wanted us dead."

"Same as here," Wren mumbled through tightly clenched teeth.

The chieftain turned aside. He chittered something to the Elder.

He turned back. "You say you come from across the sea. This could be a lie. But you do not smell as the Reds do. And you do not dress as they do. You are outsiders. Newcomers. And you speak the dragon language."

Reyna shook her head. "No. This isn't a dragon language. It's Crich. It's a language from over the ocean. Mama's first language. But we speak the Tresson language too. Some of the elves speak that. Mama made sure we knew as much as we could. Varden, too. But no one speaks that here."

The chieftain narrowed his eyes and thought. He had a word with the Elder. It was mostly in his own language, but here and there the twins caught words. Most were some combination of "great," "dragon," and "precious."

They came to an agreement, and the chieftain turned to them. "You speak of your mother. She is a Red like you, yes."

Reyna's eyes brightened and she hopped in place. "Yes! Yes, have you seen her?" she said.

The chieftain leaned close and sampled her scent. "We have. And she is a problem." He glared at Wren. "She bites as well."

"That's her!" Reyna trilled. "Is she safe? Is she hurt? Take us to her, please!"

"Follow. And behave."

The chieftain marched forward, heading for one of the many burrows that had been uncovered when the villagers emerged. The guards kept close, leading Reyna and Wren along by ropes tied to their wrist bindings. They left little slack, particularly in the case of Wren, but they weren't otherwise unkind.

Inside the burrow, the roof was low. If they had been full-grown, the twins would have had to crawl. As it was, they were able to creep along awkwardly by crouching. The Fennecs moved in the same way, but they did so with an ease and grace that betrayed a lifetime of navigating such tight spaces. The farther inside they crawled, the dimmer it got. Much of the tunnel was completely dark, but the way forward was straight, and the sound of motion echoing up and down the tunnel led the way easily enough. They did not see light again until they'd entered a larger chamber buried deep in the hill. A warm red smolder of something that looked like the charred remains of a campfire lit the place from two large bowls in the room. It left the chamber a bit warm and gave the air a sharp sting, but the acrid smell wasn't enough to hide a very familiar scent.

"Mama!" Reyna cried.

Her enthusiasm got the better of her, and she charged forward. Her personal guard yanked at the rope to hold her back.

"Behave," the chieftain repeated.

Now that all were able to stand, they moved more comfortably forward. Sections of the walls had been burrowed a bit deeper and lined with bars of the mottled red metal. This was a prison. Only the cell farthest from the entrance was in use. Two guards stood with spears ready. And trapped inside the cell was Sorrel.

They had plainly had some difficulty with her, and had reacted accordingly. The heaps of Sorrel's colorful clothing had been largely stripped away, along with the many things she hid among the layers. She was left in a ragged dress, the lowest layer of her outfit. Her hands and feet were wrapped in tightly tied sacks to keep her from clawing at the guards or attempting to unfasten the clasp of the cage. A far sturdier muzzle kept her jaws shut tight. She had her share of bumps and bruises from repeated attempts to subdue her, but the guards were in far worse shape, with fresh slashes in their fur and bandages stained with fresh blood.

It had *not* been easy keeping her captive.

Sorrel gazed out of the cell, eyes locked on Reyna and Wren as they approached. She wasn't struggling, but the intensity in her eyes was such that Reyna was astounded she'd not killed her captors with the power of her gaze alone.

"We have found your young," the chieftain said.

Sorrel's breath hissed furiously through her nostrils.

"Like you, they speak the dragon language. Like you, they are outsiders. Like you, they are Reds. Three Reds within our borders in a single day. And two more at the fringe, attempting to retrieve them. It is nothing short of a declaration of war. But they claim you are not of the Reds to the north."

She did not attempt to answer.

"They too claim you come from across the sea. It is a tale I hesitate to believe. And so you shall be treated as other captured Reds. In two days, we must make the offering. We have the wealth…" He leaned closer. "The wealth the Reds try so hard to steal… But we cannot spare the food this time. We do not have enough for ourselves and for the offering. So you shall be our token. We shall present you to your kind. We return you in exchange for enough food to make up the shortfall."

He turned and marched away from the cell. "But never before have we had to deal with children. It is a terrible thing to send your children into battle to do your bidding."

"We didn't! We weren't fighting, we were hiding!" Reyna objected.

"Behave!" the chieftain repeated. "I *should* treat them as other soldiers are treated. But I have a greater heart and a purer soul than the fiends who sent them. So I make an offer. You go willingly. You make no more trouble. And we will see to it that your children are not harmed."

He chattered to the two guards. "We shall remove your muzzle. Remember that we have your children. Act accordingly."

He motioned. The guards cautiously lowered their spears and reached through the bars. She moved forward and allowed them to unfasten the ties securing her mouth restraint.

"Now. Will you—" the chieftain began.

"You remove that muzzle from my boy," Sorrel seethed.

"First you agree to do as we say."

"You remove that muzzle from my boy, or I will tear out your throat, even if I have to do it after I'm dead." She clasped the bars with her bound hands. "I do not answer a question or do a thing you tell me until you take that muzzle from my boy."

She spoke Crich, her native language, and thus spoke with a fluidity and clarity that had been missing as she taught her children Tresson.

"He bites," the chieftain said.

"Of course he bites! You tied him up. You pulled him underground. You would bite too." She looked to Wren. "Wren, they will take off the muzzle. When they do, do not bite. It is better to behave and have some freedom than to snap and have none."

He nodded and muttered through the muzzle, "Yes, Mama."

"I did not agree," the chieftain said.

"You do not agree, then I do not agree." Sorrel turned her head aside. "I will not do what you say. I will fight you every time you give me the chance. You have to choose which you want. A muzzle on my boy and an enemy of me, or no muzzle on my boy and a chance to speak calmly."

The chieftain grinned. "She makes orders and demands, even behind bars. The Reds do have spirit. Take the muzzle from the boy."

Wren's guard pulled at the ties, and the muzzle fell away.

"I'm sorry I couldn't keep Reyna safe, Mama," Wren said.

"Don't apologize for that, Wren. That was never up to you. Reyna learned the same lessons you did. She can care for herself just as well as you can." Sorrel's expression hardened. "You should be sorry *you* got caught. And the same goes for her. And for me as well." She crossed her arms. "It is like I've said. There is always someone faster or smarter."

"Let us speak, Red," the chieftain said. "Will you do as I say if I promise that your children will be safe?"

"Say what you wish to say, and I will answer honestly, but I will not promise to do a thing that I cannot be sure I can do. Not with the safety of my children at stake."

"I plan to take you to the offering. I ask that you behave yourself until then. I ask that you speak to your people on the day of the offering and request that they share their bounty in exchange for you and your children being returned to them."

"They are not my people."

"You are a Red."

"I am a malthrope. And yes I am red. But they are not kin. I matter no more to them than I matter to you."

"You speak the dragon language. That means you have value. Do not lie to me."

"I do not lie. Why would I lie? You will meet them soon and learn the truth." She turned her head haughtily. "You will not trick me into saying something you can punish me and my children for. I am not a fool."

"Do you really value your children so little that you would maintain this falsehood even knowing what hangs in the balance?"

She thumped the bars with her bound hands. "Listen to me. You have me, yes? You have them. You asked for the truth. I am giving you the truth. If you want me to tell you the lie you already believe, then I will tell it, but you did not ask for that. You asked for the truth. I will do as you've asked. I will talk to these malthropes who look like me. But I will do it *only* if you promise that my young ones will be safe even if they do not listen to me. Because whether you believe me or not, I am an outsider. To them as well as you."

The chieftain considered her words. "You are a riddle. But I accept what you propose. You behave and you do what we ask to ensure the safety of the village. In return, you have our word that your children will be cared for and watched after as if they were our own for as long as they are in our charge."

Sorrel nodded. "Then we have a deal. Bring to me my children, please."

The chieftain nodded. Reyna and Wren were led forward. They leaned their heads against the bars, trying to rub their faces upon their imprisoned mother. She reached her bound hands between the bars and stroked their heads.

"You do what these people say," she said quietly. "You do not try to run. You do not try to fight. You do not do anything that is not safe."

"But what will happen?" Wren said.

"We do not know. We do not always know what will happen. But if there is a way for us to be together, we will be together." She nudged them. "Now go. Do not do anything that will make them change their minds unless they *already* changed their minds. And remember the game."

They nodded.

"We won the game, Mama," Wren said.

She smiled wryly. "Yes. You won the game, and I lost. When this is done, I promise you a very long story, and a very big meal. Go."

#

A few minutes later, Reyna and Wren were once again led into the cool night air. The chieftain delivered some chattered orders to the Elder who had first spoken to them, then slipped into one of the burrows.

"Your mother is trouble, but she is wise," the Elder said.

"She's the fastest and the strongest and the smartest, and you'd better not do something bad to her, or she'll teach you a lesson. And we will too," Wren warned, tears in his eyes.

"Be calm. In two days, if the Reds are as wise and reasonable as she, you will be together in their village, and we'll all be safe until the next offering."

"What happens until then? What happens now?" Reyna asked.

"There are many children without parents. You will stay with them. One guard will watch you. And you will stay tied," the Elder explained.

He hobbled along with the twins in tow and slipped into yet another of the burrows. Every hill in this place seemed to be home to a burrow. This one had a longer tunnel than most, leading deeper into the ground. Eventually, it opened into a chamber not so very different than the prison that held their mother. Fine gravel made up the floor, and a dozen or so Fennec children slept there. The Fennec young were tiny, barely larger than Wren and Reyna shortly after they were born. They wore no clothes, and as tended to be the case with malthrope young, it took a trained eye or a sensitive nose to tell them apart from a normal desert fox. The little fox kits were in a mound, piled atop each other and blissfully sleeping.

Small stakes around the edge of the room held up a short net that ringed a bed of sorts.

"Stand beside a stake. Each at a different one, if you please."

"Why?" Wren demanded.

"You will be tethered to the stake for tonight. We will untie your paws and fashion a harness. If you do not misbehave, we will see about allowing you to be without such restraint tomorrow. Hold still."

The twins looked to each other, then nodded. They held out their paws, and the guard made short work of freeing their wrists. With chatters and broad gestures, he made it clear he wanted them to turn their backs to him. Loops of rope were pulled tight around shoulders and thighs, then a rope was tied to the point where the loops met behind their backs. The guard tied a rope to each of the stakes they'd chosen. When he was through, he trudged to the edge of the room and looked upon them vigilantly.

"Sleep now. Tomorrow you will be fed, and you will join the rest of the children for their studies."

"But—" Wren objected.

Reyna held up a paw to him. He reluctantly held his tongue. The Elder nodded and took his leave.

Wren stared at the guard with a vicious gaze for a full minute before he turned to Reyna again. She was tugging gently at the rope that tied her, testing its strength.

"We need to find a way out of here," Wren said in Tresson.

"Do you think they'll get angry if we keep speaking in a language they don't know?" Reyna replied quietly.

"I don't care. If I don't say what I'm thinking, I'll never last." He looked to the armed Fennec at the door. "The guard is a rotten old fool who looks as ugly as he smells."

With ears like his, even if Wren had whispered it, there was no doubt he would have heard. The insult failed to produce any reaction, but it made Wren smirk.

"You should try it," he said, crawling over to her until he ran out of slack. "It makes you feel a little better."

Reyna crawled toward Wren as well, and at the very end of each of their ropes they were just near enough to touch one another. She used this freedom to give him a slap in the back of the head.

"That was a dangerous thing to do!" she said. "Even if he can't understand. That's misbehaving. We are supposed to behave, or they will hurt Mama."

He gritted his teeth and rubbed his head. "They are going to hurt Mama anyway. It's like she says: if someone can hurt a malthrope, they will hurt a malthrope. So we must make sure they can't."

"But *these* are malthropes. If we can't trust them, who can we trust?"

"We can't trust *anybody*. Mama says that too!" He sniffed and looked to the guard. "He doesn't look so tough. But they're sure fast. Even if we could get loose, I don't know if we could beat him without one of us getting hit with that sword."

"And we'd still be in this place, surrounded by them. And they'd still have Mama. I think we have to wait. At least until morning. We should learn more. Maybe we'll learn something we can use."

He nodded sullenly and flopped onto the ground to curl up for the night.

"Why is it always thinking and watching and learning?" he pouted. "Hunting and fighting are so much simpler."

"We don't get simple things," Reyna said, curling up against him as best she could. "That's what makes us stronger than the ones who *do* get simple things."

Though it may have been the first time in their lives that Reyna and Wren slept among their own, in the midst of a city and with a roof over their heads, it was the coldest, loneliest moment of their lives. Never before had they been forced to endure an entire night away from their mother. It was chilling, a sour and hollow feeling. They may as well have lost a part of themselves. If not for exhaustion, they might not have slept at all. But they'd not had a proper meal that day and they'd been awake from dawn to nearly dawn again. Their little bodies simply gave out, slipping into a fitful slumber.

Chapter 5

After what felt like moments, a voice caused Reyna to sluggishly blink awake. At some point during the night the Fennec kits had discovered there were newcomers. They'd made their way over and curled atop and around the twins, adding them to the sleep pile. She flicked her ears and slowly rose to a crouch, sending the three kits who had clamored atop her sliding irritably to the bedding.

She blinked more sleep from her eyes and looked in the coal-lit chamber toward the source of the voice. It was the Elder, looking as weary as she did. He was speaking in the complex chatter that formed the village's language. One by one, the kits yawned and tottered toward him to sit in a half circle before him.

The last kit to wake was the one who had curled up directly atop Wren's head. It took a direct comment from the Elder himself to finally stir the sleepy thing. In slipping from Wren's head, it woke him.

"What? What?" Wren snapped, jerking awake.

He spoke the words in Crich, and the familiar language earned curious looks from the kits.

"Oh," he muttered, realizing where he was. "*This...*"

The twins looked about the chamber. The guard that had been watching them had been replaced by a different one. In addition, aside from the kits and the Elder, a Fennec female with a small, squirming sack had entered the place. She clucked her tongue in a way that brought all of the kits scurrying eagerly to her feet, then upended the bag. A few dozen of the tiny, hopping mice that so often served as a quick snack for Sorrel and the twins here in the desert tumbled to the floor. The kits squealed with excitement and delight and bounced about to catch and gobble up as many as they could. A few made their way near enough to the twins for them to effortlessly snap them up, earning a look of admiration from at least one of the kits.

"Breakfast," the Elder said. "You have had breakfast."

The kits licked their chops and chattered among themselves. A thump of the Elder's foot drew their attention.

"Breakfast," he repeated. "You have had breakfast."

He spoke with slow care. It wasn't just the precise phrasing of someone speaking an unnatural language. It was the exaggerated elocution of someone teaching another how to speak.

"Breakfast," the kits echoed back with varying degrees of success. "You have had breakfast."

"We," Reyna said. "*We* have had breakfast."

All, including the Elder, looked to her. She shut her eyes raised her head a bit. "Mama says we should speak better than she does. Learn it right the first time."

A few of the kits, now having experienced the twins as more than simply warm heaps of fur and cloth to cuddle with, crept over to them to sniff and investigate a bit.

The Elder chattered something. Though they didn't understand the words, the twins could tell it was another lesson. Somehow it was always quite easy to tell what sort of words were being spoken for the benefit of young ears.

"Guests," he said.

"Guests," the kits repeated.

The Elder looked to the twins. "Each morning, the children learn a few words of the dragon language. And they learn the most important phrases as well. When this is through, we will discuss what we expect of you."

He tapped his foot again, and the kits gathered to him. A lesson began. Carefully phrased words echoed back, always in Crich.

"Wise… Powerful… Merciful…"

The kits parroted their teacher with little enthusiasm.

"Bounty… Offering… Benevolent…"

This final word was more than the kits could manage, and they stumbled a few times. Reyna crept forward a bit until she reached the end of her tether and repeated the word slowly.

"Ben-ev-o-lent," she said.

Wren nodded. "Smaller pieces are easier. Ben."

The kits peered curiously back and forth between the twins and the Elder. He gave them an encouraging nod.

"Ben," they mimicked.

"Ev," Reyna said.

"Ev."

"Oh," Wren said.

"Oh."

"Lent," they said together.

"Lent."

"Ben-ev-o-lent," said the twins.

"Ben-ev-o-lent."

"Benevolent," they said with clarity.

"Benevolent," the kits replied.

"Good. This is good." The Elder chattered a bit to the kits, then addressed the twins. "You would be well served to learn what I say next. It should be easy for you, and it will help you if you find a home with us."

He took a breath and recited something. It had a singsong cadence, and the way he delivered the words was unnatural and without flavor or life. It was as though the individual words were not intended to be taken separately. It was simply a long, complex thing, spoken in full, and devoid of sincerity. He paused regularly, giving the kits the opportunity to repeat what had been said thus far.

"Oh Boviss. You who are so wise. We present to you these offerings. May they nourish your mighty body and add to your legendary glory. May they earn for us mercy until the next full moon," he said.

The kits did well enough in repeating the odd little prayer, then fidgeted until a nod dismissed them. They scampered into the tunnel and out toward the heart of the village. The twins, still tethered to their stakes, remained. He approached them.

"You speak the dragon's language very well, for two so young. The Reds must be training you to oversee the offering."

Wren shook his head. "It's all from Mama. What even *is* the offering?"

The Elder regarded them dubiously. "You cannot have survived to even so tender an age without knowing of the offering."

"We're not from here," Reyna said. "We've said it over and over. We're from across the sea."

"But surely Boviss's influence is without boundaries."

"What's a Boviss?" Wren said angrily. "You say these things like we should know them. It's your stupid—"

Reyna slapped his head.

"It's your *strange* custom, not ours," Wren said, rubbing at where he'd been struck.

The Elder beckoned for the young female who had fed the kits. He chattered with her a bit, and she nodded and hurried into the tunnel.

"You have had a very strange life, or you cling to a lie more firmly than I had imagined. Either way, the village cannot afford to support newcomers unless they can make themselves useful."

Wren's head perked up. "I can hunt! Send me to hunt." He tugged the tether. "Take off this tether, and I'll get something big and tasty for all of us."

"Not alone. Not when we do not know that we can trust you not to escape."

Wren leaned aside to his sister and muttered in Tresson, "It was worth a try."

"Sometimes it takes a child's mind to know how best to speak to another child's mind. You are young, but you know the dragon language. If you will help to educate the kits, you will be fed, and you will be taught the things you claim not to know."

"We just have to teach them words?" Reyna said.

"And help them to understand."

"And you'll feed us and keep us safe?" she asked.

"We shall treat you as we treat our own young. At least until the time of the offering. If your people do not take you back on the day of the offering, we shall do so for as long as we are able."

"What about Mama?" Wren asked. "She's a very good teacher. The best. She taught us to speak, and she taught us the game. She could teach these kits better than any of us."

"Your mother has another role. One that cannot be altered."

"What are you going to do with her?" Wren demanded.

The Elder signaled to the guard. He carefully untied the twins and gathered their tethers.

"To understand that, you must understand the first and most important lesson…"

#

The Elder led the way into the light of the sun, the twins in tow and the guard a short distance behind.

"This village is one we call simply Burrow. If it is not home to the *whole* of the Fennec tribe, it is home to the bulk of it. Few who live beyond the borders of our village live long. And none of the Fennecs who venture far from our territory return. We have been spared the ravages of the world, but it comes at a price."

"The ravages of the world?" Wren said.

"There are elves to the south who mean us harm. There are dwarves in the mountains, and deep in the ground who resent that we mine as they do."

"So people hate you here," Reyna said. "Just like everywhere."

"We are hated. But here, we are safe. Because no one, not a dwarf, not a human, not an elf, will venture into this place, for fear of what will become of them at the claws of Boviss."

"But what *is* Boviss," Wren asked impatiently.

"Boviss is a dragon. Old as the mountain, and nearly as large. He is invincible. He is all-knowing. He is mightier than an army, and swifter than the wind. His breath could turn the desert to glass. It could boil the sea to salt. He brings a swift and terrible end to any who enter his domain, save the malthropes."

"There's one creature in the world that likes malthropes, and he's a dragon?" Wren said.

"He does not like us. If it were his whim, he would char us to cinders. But generations ago, he came to the leaders of the Fennec tribe and the Red tribe, and he made an offer. He would tolerate us within his domain, and we could live in the protection of his terrible shadow, if we offer to him gifts of our bounty when the moon is full. He demands meat. And he demands gold and jewels. If we satisfy his needs, he leaves us be. If we do not, penalties must be paid."

"What does this have to do with Mama?" Reyna asked.

"Your mother is a Red. We shall offer to return her to the Red tribe in exchange for enough meat to make the offering."

"Why can't you just get your own meat?" Wren said.

"And why would they give it to you in exchange for Mama?"

"Many times we have captured Reds. Always they have been in search of our mines, or to steal from our stores. You see, while they have more food than they could ever need, food enough to easily make their offering to Boviss, they have little means to acquire the gold he seeks. We have quite the opposite problem. The desert's bounty can support the village, but there is seldom meat of the quality or quantity to satisfy Boviss. So they try to rob us. We try to rob them. And if one side catches the other, trades can be made."

"Why don't you just trade gold for meat then?" Reyna asked. "If they have so much of one and you have so much of the other."

"That is not Boviss's bidding. He demands offerings to prove we are worthy of his mercy. He expects us to acquire them by force or by labor."

"How would he know?" Wren asked.

The Elder lowered his head. "He knows all."

"Wh-what happens if the Reds don't take us and Mama?"

"If they take your mother but refuse you, you will be raised among us. There may be some advantage to having some Reds among us, if you can truly come to be trusted. You will help teach the kits. When you are stronger, you will work beside us to pull gold and jewels from the earth for future offerings. Reds are strong. You would mine well."

"What if they don't take Mama *and* they don't take us?" Reyna said.

"Penalties will be paid, because we don't have enough food to offer Boviss for this moon."

"What penalties?"

The Elder shook his head. "That is not something to trouble young minds. Come. I will show you to the other caretakers. You seem not to know the proper language of your people. You should learn."

#

And so the time began to pass within the village of Burrow. Reyna and Wren did as they were told. Meals were small and rare, but they were at least assured. And after years of traveling alone and a lifetime of hearing of other malthropes only in the tales their mother told, they were with their own kind. The air was filled with the scent of their own. Until now, a village was a place requiring great caution. They had been through a few, mostly the elven ones farther south, but they could only linger briefly. Those were alien places. They were built for other sorts of creatures. Built to keep *out* creatures like Reyna and Wren. This? This was a place *for* them. In truth it was just as alien to them, but it didn't *feel* alien. It felt like a home. This was how malthropes lived. Or, at least, how malthropes were meant to live.

It took a bit of an adjustment, staying in the same place for so long, but at least the time was filled with tasks to keep their minds off the fact that their mother, and to a lesser degree they themselves, were prisoners here. The Elder requested that they stay with the kits and help teach them the trickier words in the Crich language. Thanks to the Fennec children's smaller breed, the twins had a hard time determining just how old they were. They *looked* like infants, but they moved and behaved more like they were just a bit younger than Reyna and Wren. The little ones learned slowly, but that was no surprise. Though the people here believed this was a dragon language, Sorrel had taught them that it was mostly spoken by humans. The sounds were difficult to form with a malthrope's mouth. But as with anything, a bit of dedication and practice was all it took to master the language.

The education wasn't a one-way street, either. While Crich was a mouthful for a malthrope, whatever language the Fennecs spoke to one another was simplicity by comparison. The chatters and chitters were made for long tongues and pointed muzzles. Reyna in particular was fascinated by the sounds. Whenever she didn't have a task assigned, she would sit with her eyes shut and drink in the music of the language. The meaning eluded her. A dozen conversations going on at once wasn't the best way to learn to speak a language. But by the end of the first day in the village, Reyna found herself longing for a chance to add this to the pile of languages Sorrel had taught.

Her favorite times, though, were when she caught a glimpse of the fairies. She and Wren were no strangers to the creatures. When one lives one's life where humans and their like can't or won't go, one tends to cross paths with the more mysterious and mystical inhabitants of the world. But until now, fairies were just a rare and interesting scent on the wind and buzz in the air. She'd only ever seen one as an uncertain glimmer in the distance or darting out of sight. Here they drifted through the village as though they belonged there. Reyna supposed they did.

Wren was equally fascinated by the place and its people, but his interest fell elsewhere. He and his sister weren't the only ones who were learning to hunt and hide. They had their own version of the game here, and it was something of a wonder to see it played. Many of their lessons took place down in the burrow where the kits slept. While he and Reyna repeated tricky words like "mercy" and "fealty" for young mouths to imitate, a darkened passage nearby echoed with scratches and sniffs. While Sorrel focused on running, being mindful of the wind, and finding a scent while hiding one's own, the Fennecs learned quite different skills. Here, digging was key. Wren watched in awe as a creature barely his size illustrated to eager students how to dig a tunnel faster than he'd imagined possible. They learned how to navigate in darkness. Little games and tests taught them to judge how far to dig, and how to find things lurking beneath the surface.

And then there were the weapons and tools. Sorrel knew her way around a needle and thread, but for everything else they needed—and it was precious little—they "found" them among humans, elves, and the like. These people made their own. Now and again a Fennec stinking of smoke dashed into the village toting a bundle of hammered blades. Wren caught a glimpse of people sprinkling sand on strips of cloth, then rubbing and grinding at weapons until their edges gleamed.

By many measures, the time in that village was some of the best of their lives. They were safe. They weren't lonely. Each had new things to learn, and new jobs to do. And they finally knew that there was a place where their kind thrived. But it was all tempered by the worry and sadness of knowing that they lacked their freedom. More often than not, they had their harnesses in place. They always felt the gaze of guards. And they were not permitted to see their mother. While they worked, learned, watched, and listened, Sorrel was caged. It was a cruel darkness that hung over this wondrous time of discovery.

And for better or worse, it was nearing its end.

#

Two days had passed slowly for Sorrel. When her children had been taken away again, they had replaced the muzzle, and kept it in place whenever she wasn't being fed. Sorrel couldn't blame them. Half of the soldiers in the village were nursing wounds in the shape of her powerful jaws. But without the means to speak, and with her hands and feet rendered clumsy by their bindings, she was left with little to fill the time but worry about what might be happening to her young ones. She breathed in long, slow whiffs, scouring each breath for the scent of Reyna and Wren. She seldom got so much as a hint of them. The burrows were clearly dug with the precise intent to keep scents from reaching the surface so that the place could be hidden even from those with a malthrope's senses. This meant she was treated only to the smell of her captors and of the stinking coal lamps they used.

At least, such had been the case until a few hours earlier. She'd been more carefully bound and hauled to the surface, where a rather ornate round cage fashioned of the same metal as their weapons had been readied for her. It was sized for a Fennec, not someone with her long, lean frame, so Sorrel was uncomfortably cramped as she was locked inside and hefted onto a sledge like cargo.

All of her bonds were still in place, but just getting a whiff of clean air and taste of the sun again felt like freedom. Then, like a bolt of lightning, she was hit by the scent of her little ones. Her eyes locked upon the doorway of a burrow on the opposite side of the village. She heaved herself against the bars, nearly upsetting the cage. The guards surrounding her chattered angrily. A few days of hearing them barking warnings and talking among themselves had taught her little of what their words meant, but much of their tone. Threats rained down upon her, but she was quite beyond heeding such things. The two days with only a glimpse of her children was an eternity, far worse than any torture might have in store for her if she continued to misbehave.

Sorrel wrapped her bound hands around the bars and shook them, growling muffled demands that reached the world only as angry hisses through her nostrils. The guards drew spears and swords. From the way they brandished them, this heavily bound, caged creature was every bit as frightening to them as a wild beast set loose in their village. The ornately dressed chieftain emerged and rushed to them. He issued some direct and very angry orders to his guards, then looked to Sorrel.

"Calm yourself. They are being summoned," he said.

The bars practically creaked under her grip as she glared at the chieftain.

"I have young of my own," he said, as though the words should calm her. "I know that you would do anything in your power to keep your children safe. What I do today, I do for that very reason."

He swept his hands at the cage. "This brings me no joy. But if we allow your people to enter our lands, soon we will not have what we need to keep the good favor of Boviss. And without him, we lose all."

With the muzzle in place, Sorrel couldn't reply. That was just as well. The words she had in mind were best left unsaid, particularly to one's captor.

Motion at the edge of the village drew her attention, and once again her body heaved against the bars. She couldn't have kept still if she'd wanted to. Reyna and Wren were trotting toward her. They would have been sprinting if not for the leashed harnesses in the hands of guards struggling to keep them back.

"Mama!" they called.

The guards managed to hold the twins just far enough from the cage to keep their grasping fingers from reaching the bars. Sorrel breathed in their scent like a thirsty traveler getting her first grateful gulp of water at an oasis. Anger sizzled beneath the surface to see them tied like animals, but the anger was tempered by the profound relief that they were unharmed. They were clean. They were fed. The Fennecs had even provided some sand-colored robes to replace the ratty cloaks Sorrel hadn't had a chance to repair.

"Where are you taking her?" Wren demanded.

"Take us too!" Reyna insisted.

Sorrel jabbed at her muzzle, doing all that she could without words to demand it be removed.

"You will not be freed from your muzzle," the chieftain said.

Narrowing her eyes at him, she leaned back, then yanked herself against the bars again. The cage teetered. A second well-timed shove sent the whole heavy metal prison tumbling down. It clanged hard against the ground and upset the sledge. The rest of the offering scattered about. Had he not sprung aside, the chieftain would have been struck by the falling cage. As it was, Sorrel found herself rather painfully resting on her side in the toppled prison.

"Mama!" Reyna cried.

Guards gathered around the cage, blocking her view of her children. The chieftain emerged from between them. He crouched to address her. Her fallen position finally gave him the opportunity to look down upon her.

"Do you really think this will do you any good?" he fumed. "Have I not made it clear that your own life and the lives of your children are in *your* hands? You behave yourself and they will be treated as well as my *own*. If your fellow Reds are willing to take you in exchange, in a few days you will be among your own again, with them by your side. It is better than you deserve for encroaching upon our land."

Sorrel didn't pay his words any heed. She was too busy grinning behind her muzzle as she heard the commotion going on behind the row of guards. The chieftain noticed just a moment too late. Amid shouts from his guards, two forms came bursting through the wall of Fennecs. Wren bounded over their heads. Reyna wove between them. Wren came down on top of the cage and slashed his claws at the guards around his mother. Reyna slid to a stop outside the cage and reached through, her cunning fingers working at the bindings of her muzzle.

The Fennec guards worked quickly. Wren did his best to intimidate them away. He even tangled with one. But sheer numbers and better weapons meant Wren had to submit or face the bite of their blades. The twins were hauled away. More angry orders were relayed back and forth. When they were secured and back out of sight, the chieftain spat vicious words while his people loaded Sorrel and the sacks of gold and gems atop the sledge once more.

"We have held many of your kind as prisoner awaiting the day of the offering. *Never* have we held anyone so unwilling to listen to reason. Fine. If you must act as a feral mongrel, you will be treated as one." He turned to his men. "Cover the cage. She shall have no light and no fresh air until the journey is through. And her children remain here. I am not so foolish as to allow them another chance to free their mother by taking them along to be offered in person."

The workers were quick to obey, righting the cage atop the sledge and lashing blankets about it to block out the sun and breeze.

"I, at least, am bound by my word. Your children are too young to suffer for the crimes you commit or the crimes they commit in your name. Whether it be with the Reds or among our own, your children shall be safe. But know that you have done little to deserve this mercy." He raised his voice. "Take her, before she can disrupt this place any further."

Sorrel felt the sledge lurch forward. She shut her eyes in the darkness and took a long, lingering whiff. There was no force in this world that could keep her from her children forever. If there was a way to find her way back to them, she would do it. But there was no telling how long it would take. She savored their scent and burned the sound of their voices into her mind. Those memories would have to sustain her, and drive her, in the days to come.

Chapter 6

Time passed. With the subdued glow of sun through the roughly woven blankets as her only indication of its passage, it was difficult for Sorrel to know just how long it had been. Hours, certainly, but the sledge moved slowly, so Sorrel suspected the journey hadn't taken them very far from the village. The baking sun on the blankets had turned her prison into an oven. Even as the light faded and the coolness of the night replaced it, the uncomfortable warmth within the cage lingered.

After an eternity, the sledge came to a stop. Fresh scents started to filter through the coarse cloth surrounding her. More malthropes. She shut her eyes and silently cursed fate. For years—indeed, for most of her life—Sorrel had lived with the growing fear that she may well be among the last of her kind. Now her nose was filled with the scent of malthropes by the dozen. This should have been a day of joy, a day of triumph. To be united with her kin, to know that they were thriving. It was a dream come true. She should have known the powers that had shaped her life into this endless struggle would find a way to strip the happiness from even this discovery.

The cage thumped roughly upright, clacking down onto a smooth stone slab. The Fennecs unfastened the ropes securing the blankets. The shroud dropped away. Though she was freed from it, the only light that reached her was the dull glow of starlight. The moon was full, but thin clouds turned its glow into an almost eldritch haze near the mountains on the horizon.

Her eyes swept over her surroundings. What little light there was shone upon a curious sight. The slab her cage rested upon was marble. It was carved with simple symbols and polished to a glassy shine. The sacks of gems and gold that had made up the rest of the cargo on the sledge had been arranged with care around her. Low, flat stones surrounded the marble slab, each carved with scenes such that they formed something of a record, a tale. She couldn't see them clearly, but most featured the hulking form of a dragon standing among burning buildings or fleeing figures.

Their journey had taken them far enough for the landscape to be noticeably different from the sandy dunes of the desert village. The land here was still arid, but grass grew in wispy tufts. The land to the north had the jagged shape of a tree line. They were at the northern edge of the desert, she supposed, where it gave way to a forest even thicker than the one to the south.

The Fennecs stood in orderly rows with the Elder and chieftain standing before them all. Smooth, flat stones pounded into the ground beside them formed a walkway leading to the slab that held Sorrel. On the other side of the walkway, a gathering of very different malthropes silently observed as the workers among them arranged another offering on a second slab.

Sorrel strained her eyes to see these more distant malthropes in detail. They were tall, lean, ranging from fiery orange to deep brown and red. She understood why the Fennecs believed these were her people. They were precisely the same sort of creature as she, at least in form. In manner, a single glimpse told of a world of difference. They stood with rigid, military discipline. Each was dressed identically, deep green capes topping leather armor. They were as heavily armed as the Fennecs, though their weaponry tended toward bows, arrows, hatchets, and cudgels. The mottled red-green metal that was so common among the Fennecs' equipment was entirely absent. Only the Red counterpart to the Fennec chieftain wore any metal at all, in the form of a small dagger at her belt that looked to be ceremonial in purpose.

The village leaders approached one another. Sorrel pivoted her ears and listened intently. They chattered at one another, both speaking the same language with markedly different intonations. Sorrel didn't need to know the meaning of their words. From their body language alone, she could see that a negotiation was taking place. Broad gestures swept from one carved slab to the other.

Sorrel looked to the contents of the slabs. They were as different as the villagers themselves. The Reds had offered up heaps of sumptuous foods. There were freshly killed elk and boar. Baskets overflowed with grain and fresh bread. She smelled the pungent aroma of aged cheese and smoked meats. It was a feast. But the Fennecs had offered much in the way of wealth. There was barely a glimmer of gold or sparkle of gem to be seen on the slab holding the offering from the Reds. In a clear attempt to make up for this shortcoming, elegant and ornate wood and bone carvings surrounded the bounty of food.

Meanwhile, to Sorrel's dismay, the only meat in the Fennec offering was Sorrel herself.

The debate was a brief one, and clearly did not satisfy the Fennec chieftain. He stalked back and raised his gaze to Sorrel. Despite their stormy association with one another, there was a look of regret in his eyes.

"It seems you have been truthful, at least in so far as your lack of allegiance to the Reds. They claim not to know of you. Their scouts spotted you not long after ours did. It is a pity for you that they did not reach you before we did. Then, perhaps, you might have been free among them. And a pity that they value you so little, for they were unwilling to satisfy our needs in exchange for you. There is now but one way I can serve my people. I am sorry."

#

Back at the village, Wren and Reyna watched the sky anxiously. They'd had their meal for the night, what little it was. The Elder, the chieftain, and most of the guards were off to make the offering. This left the twins in the care of younger and less experienced villagers. They were, as before, tied to a stake. Their behavior when their mother was taken away had lost them a bit of freedom. For now, at least, the stake was in the center of town some distance away from the other kits as they scampered about before bed. No one had given them any instructions, save that they should behave. And as far as they could tell, very few of those remaining in the village had a firm enough grasp of Crich to speak more than a scattering of words. All the twins could do was watch, wait, and worry.

The young male watching them was showing his inexperience. He'd turned his back to them, and from the slump of his shoulders against the butt of his spear, he might even have dozed off.

"I don't like this," Wren muttered in Tresson.

They'd been resorting to that relatively exotic language more and more while in captivity. It was as near as the pair was likely to get to privacy while still among the Fennecs.

"Mama has a plan. She must. She always has a plan," Reyna said. "We don't worry about Mama. We worry about us. *We* need a plan." She huddled a bit closer to her brother. "When you tussled with the guard, did you get anything?"

61

He grinned and gently tugged open the robe he'd been given by the Fennecs. There, tucked among his own rags, was the grip of a weapon.

"A dagger. He hasn't missed it," Wren said proudly. "What about you?"

She nodded. "When they were dragging me away from the cage. I don't know what it is, but I got this from an old Fennec."

She tucked a paw into her robe and retrieved a small ceramic bottle. It was barely the size of a large grape and had a small cork stopper on one end.

"It's just a bottle," he said. "Probably water."

Reyna shook her head. "He had water. And like Mama says, you know something is worth taking if it is worth hiding. This was hard to get."

"Open it," Wren said, bouncing a bit.

"But we don't know what it is."

"Open it and then we'll know."

They looked about to ensure there were no prying eyes, then huddled close so that the bottle was hidden between them. Reyna eased the little cork from the bottle. A subtle scent wafted from within. It wasn't water. At least, it wasn't *just* water. The odor was sweet and aromatic. Floral.

"What *is* it?" Wren wondered, taking a closer sniff. "Is this like the stuff Mama took from the bazaar in the south? The stuff for smelling nice?"

Reyna shook her head. "That smelled stronger than this. I think it might be—"

Both twins stopped suddenly as a quiet buzzing approached. They looked about to find its source, but the sound ceased as swiftly as it had begun. When they turned their attention back to the bottle, they nearly yelped in surprise.

A tiny form, not much larger than one of their paws, was standing on the ground between them. He was dressed in a papery brown tunic and flicked little wings that glittered faintly as though they'd been sprinkled with diamond dust. It was a copper-skinned, black-haired fairy. He peered up at them expectantly. Wren raised a paw, ready to swat the little fairy. It simply peered up at him curiously, completely unafraid. He lowered his paw.

"Did you come for this?" he asked, pointing at the bottle.

The fairy blinked at him, no sign of comprehension on his face.

"This?" Reyna spoke in Crich now. "Did you come for this?"

Now the fairy hopped back slightly, seemingly startled by the words. "Dragon talk," it replied in a small voice.

The twins shushed him lightly, glancing desperately about.

"Yes, dragon talk. Quiet please. Now, is this what you came for?" Reyna said.

The fairy pointed. "This."

"I don't think he speaks this language very well."

"Not speak well. Dragon talk not for Losh," the fairy replied.

"Losh? Is that you?" Wren asked.

He slapped his little chest. "Losh! Helper!" He pointed at the bottle. "Give this."

Reyna shrugged and started to tip the bottle. The fairy darted beneath it and gaped his mouth in anticipation. Wren stopped her.

"No, no. Just a little," Wren said.

She nodded and dipped a claw into the bottle. She dabbed out a sugary drop and let it fall into the waiting fairy's mouth. The fairy released a soft trill of delight as Reyna replaced the cork.

"Losh helper. Forest children need help from Losh?" He scratched his head. "Forest children... Losh helper to *desert* children. Not forest children. Goodbye, forest children!" He buzzed his wings.

"No, no! Wait!" Wren hissed.

He dropped back to the ground.

"You, uh... you are supposed to help us."

Losh shook his head. "No. Forest children I watch for. Desert children I help."

"But look at us! We're the same size as the desert children, right?" Reyna said quickly.

Confusion came over the creature's face. The twins got the distinct impression that it was not a rare expression for the simple little creature.

"Yes. Desert children big. Forest children *big* big. You, not big big." He paused for a moment. "But *red*. Forest children, red or dark brown. Desert children, yellow or light brown."

"But we talk dragon talk," Wren offered.

Losh crossed his arms. "Forest children talk dragon talk."

"And we have the *bottle*," Reyna said.

"Forest children have bottles. Not for Losh type fairy, for water fairy. But forest children have bottles."

"Think, Losh," Wren said, leaning low enough for his snout to nearly touch the tiny creature. "We are little like the rest of the village, we have the bottle that you get treats from, and we are in the village with all these people. The only *wrong* thing is our color, right?"

Losh tapped his chin, then reached out and bopped Wren's snout. "Nose too big." Losh darted up. "Ears too big. Not desert children. Forest children."

Wren tightened his jaw and snatched Losh out of the air. He spoke in an urgent whisper, teeth clenched such that they gleamed when his lips parted.

"We are malthropes. Forest children or desert children. And we gave you a treat from the bottle. And you are a helper." He tightened his grip ever so slightly and held him closer. "And we want help."

The fairy, wide-eyed, nodded. "Losh help."

The twins glanced about, then huddled even closer with the fairy sheltered between them. Wren let the little thing go, and it perched on the ground between them.

"Where do we start?" he asked.

Reyna gazed down at the fairy. "First, Mr. Losh, this is a *secret*. Don't tell anyone or call attention to anyone or anything. Understand?"

He nodded sagely. "Losh know secret."

"Good. Um… Why are there so many fairies in a malthrope village?"

"Helpers."

"Yes, but *why*?" Reyna said.

Losh pointed to the bottle. "This."

"You do it just for this stuff?"

The fairy shook his head. "No. Also because helping is good. A good thing to do. Not all fairies can help."

"How do you help?"

"Hiding. Hiding smell. Hiding trail. Hiding *everything*."

"How can you hide someone's smell?"

"Losh show?"

"No!" Wren said. "They'll see. This is secret, remember."

Losh nodded. "Secret. So… words? Show with words?"

"Please," Reyna said.

"Losh…" The fairy waved his hands. "Losh take… wind…" He slumped. "Losh words not good. Not good dragon talk."

"Fine. Do you know where they took our mother?" Wren asked.

"Mother. Child of forest? In cage?"

"Yes."

"To dragon. For dragon day. To trade."

"To the Reds? The forest children?"

Losh nodded. "Or dragon."

"They might trade her to the dragon," Reyna said coldly.

"Dragon day *for* giving to dragon."

Wren's words were heavy with a potent mix of fear and anger. "If they… if they give her to the dragon, what will the dragon do with her?"

Losh shrugged. "Dragon things."

"*What* dragon things?" Reyna urged.

The fairy counted off the answer on his fingers. "Dragons burn. Dragons eat. Dragons keep. Dragons… just burn, eat, and keep."

Reyna and Wren looked at him in horror.

"D-do you now where this is happening?"

"Dragon place!" Losh said brightly.

"Do you know how to get there?"

Flitting up proudly, he said, "Losh know all the wheres and all the hows of going."

They looked to one another again. It took no more than a moment of eye contact for the twins to know that they were of one mind. There was only one thing to be done, and only one time to do it. Wren pulled the stolen blade from where he'd hidden it. Losh flitted back slightly.

"Losh, we want two things from you. We want you to show the way to this dragon place, and we want you to do like you do for the others, keep us secret when we go."

Losh nodded, then held up a finger. "Losh keep forest children secret, if forest children keep forest children secret."

A voice called out from the edge of the courtyard where the twins were kept. Reyna couldn't understand the words, but there was suspicion in the tone. Finally, someone wise enough to suspect two prisoners huddled together and whispering might be up to something had taken notice.

"Don't worry. We'll move as secretly as we can," she said. "Let's go."

Wren nodded and slashed the ropes that held them. In a flash of motion so quick Losh had to scramble to keep up, the twins bounded into the air and sprinted for open dunes surrounding the village.

A call of alarm rose up around them, but with so many members of the village off overseeing the offering, there weren't enough of them to stop two young and very motivated malthropes. The twins burst out into the open and dashed for all they were worth. Though the Fennecs couldn't keep them from escaping, they were easily a match for Reyna's speed and only a shade slower than Wren. He couldn't very well leave his sister behind, and for a few harrowing moments, the fleeing pair and their recruited fairy were just a few healthy strides from being recaptured.

Then Losh put his skills to work. He may not have had the words to explain how he helped the Fennecs hide, but he most certainly had the means to show them. A powerful and precise wind kicked up. Regardless of which way the wind had been traveling when they'd begun, it now rushed from behind, drawing the scent of their pursuers to their noses and keeping their own scent from those who followed. At this range, that was scarcely of any help, but the same wind picked up the powdery sand that topped the dunes and swirled it into the air. It billowed into great trailing clouds until a glimpse over their shoulders showed only a wall of sandy debris.

If they couldn't see those on their trail, then they couldn't *be seen* either. That was all the twins needed. They made a sudden shift in direction. Losh followed. His buzzing flight took him down to the ground. He started bouncing across the surface of the sand like a stone skipping across a pond. Though he was a tiny thing, each time he struck, the ground rattled like a boulder had been dropped. The rumbling continued long after he flitted up again, and redoubled each time he struck.

For a moment, Reyna and Wren thought he was trying to trip them up, but when they looked down to see what he was up to, they realized that the rattling of the ground was causing their footprints to sift down to smooth sand again. By the time the whirling wind was done with their path, it looked like any other stretch of sand.

No footprints, no scent trail, and a cloud of dust keeping them from being seen. No wonder these creatures were able to sneak up so effectively. In the space of minutes, the evasive path and the mystic efforts of the fairy had allowed the twins to vanish into the desert with no sign of the pursuers.

"Losh show," the fairy crowed, realizing the first of his jobs was done and now eager to get to the second.

They dashed north, following the fairy, who now and again thumped the ground to wipe their trail away.

"When this is over," Wren puffed, "we need to try to get our own fairy."

Reyna nodded, panting in her efforts to keep up. "They're *very* nice."

#

Voices among both Reds and Fennecs called out. The Fennec chieftain raised his eyes to a swath of the sky that had grown still darker.

"Boviss approaches. Know this. It brings me no joy to do what must be done. But rest assured, your children will be cared for. I wish things could have been different."

He stepped back and joined his people. Sorrel growled and shook the cage. Now atop a firm, stable platform, she had no hope of tipping it. With few other options, she poured her frustration out into the stout metal bars regardless.

A distant sound, unlike any she'd heard before, rushed over the landscape. It was vast and airy. As it drew nearer, Sorrel realized it must be the regular, whistling flaps of wings greater than the sails of a frigate. She twisted in her prison, searching for the source. Before she saw it, she felt it. Great gales of wind surged across the altar, spilling some of the carefully arranged offering. The scattering of buzzing fairies in the malthrope entourage fought to keep from being blown away.

Finally, she turned enough to see the creature they had assembled to honor. Sorrel shuddered at the sight of him. She had seen dragons before. Always from afar, and only briefly. They were enormous creatures, fearsome and powerful. But those she had seen were nothing in comparison to this… *thing*.

The elephant-sized dragons she'd assumed were the largest of their kind would scarcely stand at chest height to Boviss. Just one of this vast wings could cast the whole of the Fennec village in darkness. Titanic jaws held teeth longer than spears. His head was a wreath of horns and fins that could turn away siege weapons. Gouges and slashes covered his hide, evidence of a thousand battles. They were all shallow, glancing blows shrugged off in years gone by. None was so deep as to truly be called a scar. It was possible that this beast had not once shed a drop of its own blood.

It was right to worship this monster. It was right to do anything that would keep him from burning you to ash.

All in attendance raised their hands and lowered their heads.

"Oh Boviss. You who are so wise. We present to you these offerings. May they nourish your mighty body and add to your legendary glory. May they earn for us mercy until the next full moon," they chanted in one voice.

The dragon's great head angled down to inspect the offerings made by the Reds. What had moments ago seemed like a feast fit for a village now looked to be barely more than a mouthful. He sniffed at the heaps of food and flicked at them with his great tongue.

"You hunt well, forest children," rumbled the dragon in a voice like distant thunder. "Your offering of food pleases me."

He leveled his eye with the slab, tilting his head to do so. The dragon's eye was set so deep in his armored skull that it was little more than a glimmer in the darkness. Even so, one could see the dismissal and judgment as it studied the scrimshaw and carvings.

"What is this?" he rumbled.

The chieftain of the Reds stepped forward and cast her eyes low.

"Oh great Boviss. We have scoured our lands for all things precious, but though the forest offers much, it does not—"

"Did I ask you for excuses, Child of the Forest?" Boviss asked.

This time, Sorrel felt something new when the dragon spoke. There was a crackle beneath his voice, the stink of brimstone on his breath, and the smallest flare of orange deep in his throat.

"No, oh great Boviss."

The dragon sat, shaking the very earth beneath their feet, and held out a massive claw. He scooped up a wooden statue. It was nearly life-size, a depiction of what must have been a fabled warrior of the village. The detail was striking, the design superb. Such a statue must have taken thousands of hours to craft. In Boviss's grip it may as well have been a figurine.

"What is this?"

The Story of Sorrel

"It is the thing of greatest value that we have to offer. It was crafted in your name by our greatest artisans. There isn't another like it in the—"

Boviss tightened his claws. The masterpiece was reduced to kindling with a soft splintering crunch.

"I do not care what *you* value. And you *know* what I value. Have you nothing more to offer?" He flicked one of the bone carvings aside like an unwanted crumb from his plate. "Because if you do not, your obligation to me is only half-filled."

The Red chieftain trembled lightly and lowered her head farther. She pulled the gold chain from her neck and held it out.

"This is the chain of my station. It has been passed from leader to leader since even before you deigned provide us your protection. I offer it."

She held out the gold chain. Boviss dumped the shreds of the carving on the ground and hooked the chain with a claw. From his point of view, it was barely a thread.

"Open your ears, Child of the Forest. I do not wish to repeat myself again. What carries value for you does not carry value for me. The years mean nothing for me. They are a blink of my eye. And your traditions that stretch across those years lend no weight to this chain." He flicked it at her feet. "You have failed to meet my demands."

He craned his neck and shut his eyes. "But I am not without mercy," he added magisterially. "You have not failed for many months. I will take what you have offered, but your next offering shall be twice as large as this one should have been. If you fail, I take one of you. Of my choice."

"Yes, oh mighty Boviss." The Red chieftain bowed low, fetching her chain and retreating gratefully.

Boviss turned to the Fennec offering. His eyes fell upon Sorrel. The breath caught in her throat. She huddled down, as though somehow she could hide from him within the cage. His gaze lingered upon her, then swept across the rest of the offering. A claw stirred at the heavy sacks.

"This is proper wealth," Boviss said. "Your cousins to the north have much to learn from you, Children of the Desert. But you offer no food. Do you wish me to starve? Do you wish me to grow weak? What will become of you if I do?"

The Fennec chieftain lowered his head and dropped to one knee. "The lands are barren. The game is scarce. I would not think to insult you by offering the vermin that we feed upon to survive. But I offer you instead this captured Red."

"You offer it? Freely?" Boviss turned to the other malthropes. "Do you care so little for your kind that you would permit this?"

"The one they have captured is not of our number. She hails from elsewhere. She does not fall under our protection," the Red chieftain replied.

"From elsewhere…" Boviss murmured.

The dragon leaned low. His snout nearly touched the cage. First, a broiling hot breath, humid and stinking of smoke and flame, fluttered Sorrel's thin rags and long hair. Though she trembled, she tried to stay strong and face the beast. The breath returned as a long, deep sniff.

"Yes. She smells of other lands." He glanced at the rest of the offering, then back to Sorrel. "A rare treasure to offer, but treasures are not what your offering lacks."

The Fennec chieftain spoke, his words heavy with shame and regret. "I offer her as a forfeit. For those things we cannot offer. Use her as you see fit."

"A forfeit?" Boviss said. "You know that I take, as a forfeit, a prize of my choice." His terrible lips curled into the tiniest hint of a cruel grin. "However, of your number, I think she is the finest. I accept your offer, though she is but a morsel when I demand a meal. You, too, shall make *twice* a proper offering when I come again."

"Yes, great one. You are wise and gracious."

Boviss stood and spread his wings again. He reached out. Each of his foreclaws scraped at the slabs holding his offerings. With a skill that spoke of having done so thousands of times before, he snatched up all that was offered in his mighty grip without spilling a single nugget of gold. Sorrel released a muffled scream through her muzzle as the dim light of night was blotted out and her prison was roughly gathered into the vise-like grip. Her cage pressed tight against the sacks of gold and gems. The bars groaned and creaked under the strength of the grip. Then, in a single motion that she felt in the pit of her stomach, the beast launched himself into the sky to return from whence he came.

Chapter 7

The twins streaked through the desert. Driven by fear for their mother's safety and without cargo to haul along the way, they covered ground at twice the rate of the procession of Fennecs earlier that evening. And though Losh assured them the journey was a short one, it was still one that would take them time, and time was a luxury they did not have.

"This way! Over this way. From the next high place you will see it. Not much more," Losh said pleasantly.

"Look!" Reyna cried.

Wren and Losh followed her gaze. At first, it wasn't clear what she had seen, but slowly the dark form retreating into the sky above began to take shape in their vision. It was Boviss, already well into the sky and on his way to his lair.

"We're too late," Reyna fretted.

"Maybe the dragon doesn't have her," Wren insisted. "They said they were going to trade her to the Reds. They said that! Remember?"

"But what if they didn't?" Reyna said, eyes twinkling with tears.

"Th-the Reds and the Fennecs meet at the same place to make the offering. Right?" Wren said to the fairy.

He looked curiously at Wren.

"The forest children and the desert children!" Wren snapped.

"Yes! Yes. Always the dragon place. Always the same time."

"So they can't be far if the dragon is still so near. Can you take us to them?" Wren said.

"No."

"But you said you know all of the wheres and hows of going places!"

"Losh did not say the *whos* of going places," the fairy said simply.

"What do we do, what do we do?" Reyna fretted.

The twins started to rave, their voices raised and rambling.

"We find her! We've got to find her," Wren said.

"But they have fairies too, they'll hide too," Reyna said.

"So we hunt better than they hide!"

"But they beat us once! They caught us once!"

"And we got away! And we're smarter now! We learn, right? You do, at least. You're the smart one!"

"But I don't know what to *do!*"

The fairy buzzed about between them, looking with growing agitation at their faces.

"Why is sad? Why yell?" Losh said, suddenly anxious. "Losh helper! Losh help!"

"We don't know where she is. And if she's with the dragon—" Reyna squealed.

"If she's with the dragon, then we'll slay the dragon. Mama taught us to be strong. We'll do what we need to do," Wren said.

"You think being strong is all it takes, but we're not stronger than a dragon!"

"You don't know that! We never fought a dragon. There's probably a secret way to beat them. Swift would know how to beat a dragon."

"Swift isn't real!"

The fairy flitted between them and released a piercing, high-pitched chirp that caused both the twins to wince.

"No yell," he said firmly. "Losh no like yell."

They blinked a bit and took some deep breaths. Reyna shut her eyes tight and tried to put her frenzied mind to work.

"There's a way forward. There's always a way forward. Mama is either with the Reds or with..." She shuddered. "The dragon. If she's with the Reds, we just need to go to them. If she's not, that means she's with the dragon."

"And if she *is* with the dragon, then we'll need help. And we can only get that help from the Reds," Wren said.

"Help? They won't fight a dragon for us," said Reyna.

Wren had already turned to the north and begun sampling the air. "We won't know until we try. We've already been with the Fennecs, and they traded Mama away. They had us prisoner. We had to escape from them."

Reyna considered his words. "I suppose it is the best we can do for now."

"So we go to the Reds," Wren said. "I think I have their scent..."

"Losh not go to forest children place," the fairy said. "Losh help desert children."

"Oh… Well, thank you for your help." Reyna rummaged through her things and found the bottle she'd stolen. "Here. We won't need this anymore."

She set it down in the sand. Losh's eyes widened.

"For Losh? All? *ALL FOR LOSH?!*" he trilled.

Reyna nodded vaguely. She, too, had turned her attention to the breeze. Losh clutched his hands and spun in a circle.

"Losh help desert children. Always. Forest children, never. But…" He clapped his hands. "Names!"

"What?"

"Names!" He thumped his chest. "Losh!" He flitted up and slapped Reyna's shoulder.

"Reyna," she said with a smile.

"Wren," her brother offered without further prompting.

"Reyna, Wren. Thank you. Losh not forget." He gathered up the bottle and happily darted south with it.

"What do you suppose that stuff was?" Wren asked.

"Whatever it is, he must really like it. But let's go. Maybe we can catch the Reds before they get all the way back," she replied.

#

Sorrel shivered, and not only from fear. Despite being gripped tightly in the claws of her new captor, she was not hidden from the painful iciness of the air. Wind rushed through the cage and chilled her to the bone. Now and again she caught a glimpse through the fingerlike claws that held her and the rest of his prizes, but her eyes couldn't make sense of what they saw. Churning clouds below her. The indistinct form of the land shifting by in the darkness. The one mercy of being in the clutches of such a massive and terrible creature was that it left no room in her mind to fret over something as petty as falling to her death.

After the longest few hours of her life, the wail of the wind took on a new tone. Rather than simply rushing across Boviss's wings, it whistled against stone. It was a familiar sound, the sound of the mountains. Not long after, in a moment that nearly stopped her heart, the claws gripping her cage opened. She shrieked as she plummeted through the air, then cried in pain as she and her cage struck the

73

unyielding stone. A dizzying roll and deafening sequence of clanks and thunks brought her to rest on a surface caked with ice.

The cage was on its side. The beating it had taken had bent in some of the bars and made it even more cramped. One of the bars had even been torn from its mounting on the roof of the cage. It was a wonder she'd not been skewered. Sorrel twisted and turned, trying to get her bearings.

She was in the mouth of a cave, one every bit as large as one might imagine a dragon like Boviss would call his lair. The rest of his offerings were scattered around her. Those masterpieces created by the Reds that weren't destroyed during the flight were shattered to fragments when he dropped them. A few deft swipes of his massive claws send them clattering down the mountainside like the debris he'd always considered them to be. His great tongue flicked out of his mouth and swept the sacks of gold offered by the Fennecs into his jaws. With teeth still parted, offering a glimpse of the treasure behind them, he plodded deeper into the cave.

Sorrel watched as his form vanished into the darkness of the mountain. Almost as terrifying as the monster's size was his grace. Though a thing so large should shake the mountain with its steps, Boviss plodded lightly. He was almost delicate in his motions, if such a word could be applied to a behemoth who could make a meal of most other dragons.

She shook the wonder and awe from her mind. The next few minutes could well be her last. She couldn't afford to waste even a second of this precious, unobserved time. The Fennecs had secured her well. Throughout the entire journey to the place of the offering, she'd not been able to remove either her muzzle or the sacks binding her hands. But now she had the broken bar to work with. She reached up to its jagged end and quickly tore through the sacks on her hands. When her fingers were free, she unfastened the muzzle and threw it aside.

Her unfortunate life meant she was no stranger to the various sorts of locks, latches, and clasps the people of the world used to protect their belongings. With little else to do while trapped in this cage, she'd investigated the lock that secured the door. It was a simple clasp. Sturdy enough to stay shut even after the fall, but requiring only a simple key to open. She was certain a bit of wriggling with her claw could wrench the thing open. That is, if it hadn't ended up *beneath* the fallen cage.

"Blast it. Come on," she hissed.

She grasped the bars and heaved her weight against them. The cage was every bit as heavy as she was, and it offered little room for her to move even while it was upright. She shook and lurched. The cage wobbled and clacked. She worked herself into a rhythm, each shove and thump tipping it just a bit farther. If she kept at it, she could get it to clatter over to the next set of rivets and expose the lock.

Her breathing was becoming more and more desperate. Her position had put her back to the cave, but one did not survive as long as she had without developing a sixth sense for the approach of a predator. He was coming back. Her fur stood on end as she fought harder. Desperation was the enemy of precision, though. She lost the rhythm. The cage ceased to budge. And then, time ran out.

The shadow of her captor fell upon her. All that remained for him to gather was the feast that had been prepared for him, and Sorrel herself. His great jaws opened. A skillful sweep of his tongue gathered cage and food alike into a mound. A snap of his jaws clamped the whole of the remaining offering in his maw. Great teeth creaked against the bars, threatening to skewer her if the cage didn't hold. Humid, smoky breath replaced the cold wind with searing, stinking puffs.

"No! Let me go! Let me go, *please!*" she shrieked.

A sharper rush of wind fluttered her clothes, and her head thrummed with a deafening, thunderous laugh. If he'd wanted to eat her, he could have. Cage and all, he would have no trouble sending her and half the feast stuffing his maw down his gullet. But he didn't. For now he was not devouring, he was carrying. Threads of drool oozed down between the bars as the sound of his breath and steps echoed off the walls of a deepening tunnel.

There was no sense fighting against the cage now. It was the only thing keeping her from being chomped in two. She trembled, eyes shut and teeth clenched, until the jaws opened once more. She dropped to the floor of a new chamber, and landed with a dry clatter rather than a clang. The rest of the food rained down around her.

Her heart rattled in her chest. She struggled against the bars again, hoping perhaps the teeth had damaged it enough for her to escape, but it wouldn't budge. She fumbled through the bars and felt for the clasp.

"Blast it. *Blast it!*" she cried.

The mechanism was smashed, the clasp hopelessly jammed. Even the key wouldn't be enough to free her now.

She slumped against the bars and tried to gather her wits. The dragon was moving. It padded with unnerving lightness. She could even see its massive form as a muted figure. This far into the cave, there shouldn't be any light, but there was. She searched for its source, but there didn't seem to be any torches. The glow was all around her, a faint, unnatural luminance. A tinkle of metal filled the cave. Soft cascades of nuggets clattered to the ground. Finally, a heavy thump shook the cave. She squinted and saw the vaguest form of the dragon sitting on its haunches on a mound that softly glittered in the unexplained light.

Boviss drew in a breath and released it as curling flame. It cast the chamber in warm orange light for a brief moment. Rather than simply fading away, the flame scattered like a flock of bats that swirled into points ringing the roof, sparking a dozen huge chandeliers to life.

Sorrel squinted at the sudden brightness. When her vision adjusted, she saw the truth of the chamber. This was no simple cave. It looked more like a cathedral. The floor was perfectly flat, chiseled smooth, and here and there carved with patterns and reliefs. Great stone columns with intricate designs held up a vaulted roof. And the lights that at first seemed to have been lit by the dragon's flame were arcane circles of gleaming silver, embedded with a ring of gems that smoldered the same color as the flame.

This was not a place of nature. This was a place forged over generations by the work of thousands of skilled hands. A stone statue, taller than a tree, stood to remind those who saw this place of the people who created it. And in the center, atop a sparkling hoard larger than he was, sat Boviss. His small, sinister eyes focused upon sacks mounded beside him. They must have held the most recent offering from the Fennecs. He delicately dumped their contents with the patient care of someone peeling grapes. His claw stirred the fresh dose of gems and metals and his eyes fixed on them, committing them to memory.

When he was through, his eyes turned to the food.

He stalked toward Sorrel. The light showed that the dry crackle that had broken her landing was a heap of desiccated bones. They weren't stripped of their meat. They almost looked embalmed. Food enough to feed a village, left to the cool air of the lair to shrivel and dry into husks. And tucked behind, three similar cages, twisted, broken… and empty.

Boviss sniffed at the offerings and snapped up one of the larger kills. It vanished down his gullet in a single gulp. Then the beast turned his eyes to her.

"An offering of their own flesh." He stepped closer and looked her over critically. "And a scrawny one."

"They had no right to offer me," Sorrel shouted.

Boviss raised his head a bit and looked down upon her. "Where is your muzzle, forest child?"

"I do not belong here. Those are not my people."

He narrowed his eyes and curled a lip. "I would have left you to morning. Offerings stay fresher while they still breathe. But if you are free to speak, you could be bothersome." He opened his jaws.

"You would not devour a part of your hoard, would you?" she yelped, staring down the yawning maw.

Boviss shut his mouth and gave her a steady look. "You misunderstand your role. You are meat."

"I come from across the sea! You smelled it! You in your wisdom knew to be true what my own kind did not! I am not of that village. I am not of this land at all."

The dragon lowered his snout to touch the bars of the cage and drew in another deep breath. He flicked his tongue across the cage, spritzing her with spittle.

"Indeed. Your scent is one of old memories. And so your flavor shall be a reminder of times long ago." His jaws widened again.

"You come from across the sea as well. That is not dragon talk, that is Crich. I hail from your homeland," she insisted. "We are kindred spirits. Travelers far from home."

He threw his head back in a rumbling laugh. "You suppose I have some love for my former home?" He flopped down to the ground and grinned at her. "I left that place when I was young. When the tongue was new."

"You don't speak it in an ancient way."

"Language is a simple thing. And if you think the people of the north and across the sea have kept it to themselves, you aren't as clever as you believe yourself to be. Traders bring language. Nothing that enters my domain is beyond my knowledge."

"Then… then you know how rare I am."

"A malthrope. Common. Pointless."

"A malthrope *here* is common. But across the sea? There are more *kings* than there are malthropes. The gold in your hoard is common as gravel compared to me."

Boviss tipped his head. "You think me a fool." It was a statement, spoken simply and without anger. He seemed genuinely intrigued by it. "You try to trick me, to preserve your life with this nonsense. But there is truth to your words. You are not the first to be offered to me. The others plead. The others worship. I see only terror in their eyes. But not you. You think. You scheme."

He lowered his head a bit. "You speak this language well. Not with the stumble of formality or the lifelessness of prayer."

"It is the one language I speak well."

"You are something new, then. I do not care if you are the last of the malthropes from across the sea, whether that is truth or trickery. But something new? That is something very rare indeed."

He reached out, his claws clutching about the cage. She huddled down as best she could in her prison. The bars shuddered. One by one, they buckled and deflected until the whole of the cage fell to pieces. She dropped to the uneaten offerings and shielded her face from the tumbling metal bars as they sprinkled from the dragon's claws.

Her mind moved faster than her body. She saw herself spring to her feet while the bars were still clattering to a rest. In her mind she could envision the stumble when her legs failed her after being held prisoner for days. Her imagination painted the vivid flames, searing her as she tried to escape. She saw a thousand failed escapes in those next few moments. And she saw *nothing* that didn't leave her children without a mother. And so she held still. Eyes on Boviss. Waiting.

The dragon's permanent, sinister grin widened slightly. "You did not run."

"I am awed by your splendor."

He released a single, derisive laugh. "Leave the shallow words for the others."

The Story of Sorrel

"You would have killed me if I ran."

He nodded. "Before you made a second step. I was correct. You aren't as empty-headed as the others. And that is good. There will be no room for mistakes in your life here. Having seen this place, you shall not leave it alive. But so long as you amuse me, you may yet have a long life."

He leaned lower. Smoke curled about Sorrel's face and stung her eyes when he spoke. "This way, Child of the Forest Across the Sea. Let me show you the hoard you are now a part of."

She took a step backward and swept her eyes around the lair. It was massive. Sprawling. Arched doorways led off into towering halls leading into blackness in all directions. If she ran, he would follow. Not that he would need to. A single one of his strides could match a dozen of hers, and his flame could roast her to ashes from as far away as he pleased.

"As you wish," she said, head drooping in defeat.

#

She had to hurry to keep pace with even his plodding steps. He led her past the mound of gold. Beyond it lay a grand hall littered with treasures of all sorts. The hall itself was already a masterpiece. Sturdy walls covered with dwarven designs held up arched vaulted ceilings. This was no castle. Even if its architecture made it resemble one, it was still at its core a cave, but brilliant little touches took those features of a cave that could not be carved away and made them a part of the splendor. Stone figures affixed to the roof dripped with water. Stalactites grew from their chins like beards. Grooves both above and below allowed the water to drain away with all the elegance and nuance of a fountain into grate-covered drains that funneled the water off and away.

Weapons with gleaming blades lay in haphazard piles. Gems, sigils, and runes decorated the heads of axes and the grips of spears. Some of the equipment on display was small enough to be wielded by a creature of Sorrel's size. Other pieces were massive, the sorts of things used to batter down the walls of mighty keeps.

"Many have come for me in my time. Kingdoms sent their armies to dispatch me. I crushed their warriors. Burned their wizards to ash. I trampled their castles to powder. Time has forgotten them. And all because they trifled with me."

Boviss lingered to cast a burning glare at the bolt for a ballista. "Enchantments rendered their weapons potent. For a lesser creature, perhaps they would have been enough. But I am an elder dragon. Older than the mountains. Wiser than the spirits." He lashed a rack of swords with his tail, clattering them to the ground. "I am invincible."

The dragon drew in a breath and heaved it out as flame. Fire once again swirled in the air and found its way to the hanging lights on the vaulted ceiling. Sorrel gazed at them. Like the weapons, and no doubt much of Boviss's hoard, they were works of sorcery. They fed on his flame and gave light in return. She held her fingers out and grazed them across an ax large enough to have been swung by a giant. The aura of magic was thick around it. She knew not a word of magic, but the power here was so intense she could feel it flutter against her skin and tingle in her extremities.

"Not all of those who came here sought to destroy me. Some wished to enslave me. Think of it. My might, in service of a throne. I can almost excuse their foolishness. The call of such power must be difficult to resist for those who have never tasted true strength. And they gave me one of my favorite prizes."

He gazed down at a mound of chains. If they had been intended to bind a dragon, they seemed horribly undersized for the task. The chain's links were small enough to fit in Sorrel's palm. He stirred them with a claw, unearthing a small, shriveled skeleton. The chain led to a shackle about the fallen warrior's neck. Boviss pinched the shackle with a claw and tugged it free, toppling the skull in the process.

"A wizard," he muttered. "A dwarf, as I recall. Skilled with their forges. They do so adore their prattle. He spoke for ages of this creation. No beast it cannot bind. Smelted from the bones of this creature. Infused with the tears of that creature. Their creation matters not. What matters is this."

He flicked a claw toward Sorrel. Though at his size, its tip was quite blunt, the slash was enough to gouge her skin. She recoiled in pain, but not before a fat drop of blood fell upon the coils of chain. Etched runes on every link of the chain took on a brilliant golden glow that spread along its length. The glow curled and wove along the chain in both directions until it was entirely illuminated.

Sorrel backed away as the links began to shudder. Loops of jangling chain rose up and writhed. The end with its shackle rose up. It shot forward in a viper's strike and clamped shut around her neck. The cold iron pulled tight around her. One by one, the links diminished to a scale more appropriate to bind one of Sorrel's size.

He lowered his head and grinned, great teeth gleaming.

"Welcome to my collection, Child of the Forest Across the Sea."

Chapter 8

Wren and Reyna huffed and puffed. The trail left by the Red malthropes was not a difficult one to follow. There was little evidence they had even attempted to conceal it. The last few days had been taxing for the twins. Though they seldom had real comfort or ease in their lives, Sorrel had always ensured they were well fed, and they always slept soundly when they were with her. Anxiety had wracked every moment of their day since they were separated from their mother, and living off the charity of the Fennecs made for meager meals. They'd had little proper sleep and no proper meals since the day they'd won the game. It made for slow travel.

The landscape changed around them as they trudged. The Fennecs must have made their home at the northern limits of the desert, just a few hours of travel past the place of the offering had taken the twins to grasslands. By dawn of the second day, they were deep in a forest. Now it was noon of a third day, and they were spared the punishing sun by the dappled shade of a thickening stand of fragrant fruit trees.

"We should rest…" Reyna said.

"And we need to eat." Wren breathed deep. "The air smells so good here. So heavy with game."

"No hunting," she said, sensing what her brother had in mind.

"But I could find us a deer, or a moose!" He leaned against the tree and shut his eyes dreamily. "A nice full belly. And if they *do* have Mama, she'll be so proud."

"What does Mama say? What belongs to us and what doesn't?"

"The only things that don't belong to us are the things that other people can keep from us."

Reyna nodded. "And these are malthropes. They'll be able to keep things from us if we try to take them without care."

"So I'll be careful."

Reyna tapped her chest. "I am the careful one."

He turned his head aside. "We can both be both things. That's what Mama *wants*. That's what Mama *is*."

"Even so. We are going to need help from the Reds. We shouldn't start by stealing from them."

"Then what do you want to do?"

"It smells like there is something big, not far away."

"I know," Wren said. "Just that way. I've been trying to avoid it until we can get a good look at what it is."

"Let's just go to them."

"What? We *never* just go to strangers."

"One way or another, we'll have to reveal ourselves to them. We can't ask for help in secret."

"We can try to find Mama in secret."

"Mama isn't going to be here!" Reyna snapped.

"You don't know that."

"I do know. I know that if a thing can be hard or it can be easy, for us, it will be hard. So Mama won't be there. We'll have to fight and scratch and track and jump and climb to find her. If we even *can* find her. So, just this once, let's do something the easy way. It'll be hard enough later."

Wren's expression became brittle, a layer of defiance over a pit of growing uncertainty. He must have seen the same in Reyna's eyes, because he shook himself and pulled together the shreds of his confidence.

"Maybe you're right. Maybe we *do* just walk up to them and ask for help." He grinned and dropped his voice to a whisper. "And then when they least suspect it, we *trick* them. That's what Swift would do."

"We're supposed to learn lessons from Swift, not actually do what he does, Wren."

"That's just because we're not supposed to get mixed up in the things he does. But we *are* in one of those things. We're in an adventure. So now we make like Swift."

Reyna considered his words. "*Maybe*. But let's be friendly first."

The pair nodded and wearily trudged through the trees.

#

It was oddly unnerving to be walking tall in a place where they knew others might be lurking behind every tree. The whole of their lives had been spent with wide eyes and perked-up ears. Every mile they'd traveled had been at a crouch, with the nearest hiding place always fresh in their minds. To stumble upon a footpath and choose to *use* it felt akin to walking on ice that might give way at any moment.

The Story of Sorrel

If nothing else, winding their way along the roads gave them a proper introduction to the approaching village of Red malthropes. Perhaps it was thanks to the recent trip to make the offering, but the grounds they marched through were wholly deserted. Even without skulking about, they'd yet to be seen. It was all Wren could do to keep from raiding a pen of goats they came to. In a place where the trees thinned, they found a small but thriving farm growing some manner of grain. It was not so different from the places of man they faintly remembered from before their journey across the sea, save for one very significant departure. Here, everything they encountered felt as though it belonged. No trees were felled to make room for the farmland. Crops simply found their way into this place and that. When they came upon the village itself, it was a gradual thing. There was no wall. Here they spotted what might be a door. There they spotted what might be a roof fashioned of leaves and twine.

And all the while, the felt the itchy tingle of discovery.

"We're being watched," Wren murmured to his sister.

"I know," she said.

"There's someone just behind those trees."

"I know."

"Why won't they just come forward?" he whispered through gritted teeth.

"Because it isn't every day you see two young ones dressed in the clothes of the desert village striding through our territory," came a voice from the other side.

Both twins snapped their gazes to the source of the voice and sprang aside. Sure enough, there was a Red malthrope standing not a stone's throw from the road. He was *not* the one they'd sensed. There was no threat in his posture as he took a step toward them, but Reyna and Wren couldn't fight the instinct to bare their teeth and flatten their ears.

He was dressed in simple clothing. Animal hides and lightly woven cloth. The hides kept their natural color; the cloth was dyed muted greens. Together, they faded into the forest just as naturally and effortlessly as the Fennecs' clothes suited the desert.

The stranger was tall, perhaps a bit taller than Sorrel, and had an orange color to his fur brighter even than Wren's.

He raised his hands. "Enough, enough. We've heard tell of you. The Fennecs spoke of the children who speak dragon talk better than the elders. They offered you to us in exchange for three boars. That you are here without so much as a loaf of bread in exchange suggests they don't know you're gone."

"So you didn't make the deal," Wren said. "You don't have Mama."

He stepped closer. "The procession came back empty-handed. I was not among them, but—"

"You gave her away!" Wren growled. "You could have saved her, but you let the dragon take her instead."

The malthrope crouched and spoke gently. "I cannot ask you to understand. It is not for a child to think of such things."

"What's to understand?" Reyna said. "You have so much food. You could have spared some."

"If we offer meat in trade for a captive, then when the full moon next rises, they will have more captives. We cannot reward them for offering our people in trade. Had fortune brought you to us rather than those of the desert, we would gladly have accepted you. Just as we will gladly accept you now."

He offered a hand. "Come. Much of the village is at the great hunt. After the offering, we replenish our stores."

Reyna and Wren looked to one another. As they had so many times before, they saw in that simple glance the whole of a plan form. When they turned back to their would-be benefactor, each knew what would be done. There was just the matter of doing it.

They stepped forward. Reyna accepted his hand. A second figure, the one they'd noticed but had not seen, emerged. He was in every way a match for the first stranger. Sorrel had told them that twins were quite common among the malthropes, but until this day they'd had only themselves to stand as examples. He offered a friendly smile and extended a hand to Wren, who took it somewhat more reluctantly.

"This way," said the first stranger. "And welcome to your new home."

#

For nearly an hour, Reyna and Wren were treated to a place they would not have imagined in their wildest dreams. They saw cozy homes fashioned among the trees. They smelled fresh bread baking. They saw clothes being sewn and art being carved. Most of all, they saw others of their kind. Not hiding. Not suffering. They'd seen the

Fennecs during their time there, but seeing these creatures that looked so much like them, so much like their mother and their father, made it even more magical. And they weren't huddled and struggling like the Fennecs. The air was thick with the scent of families living their lives without fear of discovery. Here and there, as had been the case in the Fennec village, fairies buzzed about. They mostly congregated around a spring that flowed through the center, their merry trilling and shimmering glow adding a joyous radiance to the place.

The twins who led them were named Hask and Kell. They moved with an easiness and openness that seemed almost unnatural for a malthrope. This, it seemed, was what a malthrope could be if he allowed his guard to drop. Graceful steps took on an almost musical cadence. Pointed muzzles curled into comfortable grins. All who called this place home were well fed and unafraid. Things were just *simple* here. Even the Fennecs had the sense of desperation to their lives. That there could be a place like this for people like Reyna and Wren made their lives before feel like a cruel trick.

"Are you hungry?" Hask asked. "Would you like something to eat?"

He was the first of the twins they'd met, though since that moment it had ceased to matter. The two were in all ways interchangeable.

"Yes please," Reyna said politely.

"Sit. Kell shall fetch you something," he said.

The pair obediently sat on the soft moss of the forest floor.

"So the Fennecs claim you are from across the sea. Is this true?"

Wren nodded. "We came when we were littler. With Mama." The young malthrope's words and posture still had an edge to them.

"A dangerous journey. We'd believed there were none of us left in that land."

"There aren't," he said.

"Except for Papa," Reyna corrected. "And we didn't know there were any malthropes here either."

"If not for Boviss, by now there may not have been. But his grace defends us and makes all of this possible."

"He took my mama," Wren fumed.

Hask lowered his head. "The price he asks is great. We have lost many to him, when the earth has not been as open with its bounty as the forest has been. But to lose some is better than to lose all."

Kell returned with two healthy cuts of meat. He presented one each to the children. He also not-so-subtly held something sweet-smelling wrapped in cloth. "For after," he said, patting the cloth.

Reyna and Wren tore into the red, raw meat they were offered. It was divine, the tenderest part of a fine, healthy beast. Just what beast it was, they had no clue. Certainly something they'd never had the good fortune to capture on their own. Whatever it was, it was marbled with fat and drenched with flavor. Both brothers sat before the children and watched happily as short work was made of the food.

"We were talking of the price that must sometimes be paid to Boviss," Hask informed his twin.

"Yes. Of course. Just the subject we hoped to discuss," Kell said.

Wren wiped his mouth, already finished. "Why would you want to talk about that with us? All we know about Boviss is he's big and he scares everyone." He added with a drop of venom. "And you let him take Mama."

"Then you know all you need to know," Hask said. "You know the terrible price that must be paid if his offering does not satisfy him. We were fortunate that he was merciful. We had but one mine, and it has run dry. We have no gold, no jewels. Even the amber pit hasn't provided a gem in months. And now Boviss requires twice his price to make up for our shortfall."

"There is not wealth enough in the entire forest to satisfy that demand," Kell explained.

"So what can we do?" Reyna asked.

"You have seen what few of us have ever seen. You have been among the Fennecs."

"So?" Wren asked.

"You know of their wealth. You know of the bounty of their mines," Hask said.

"It isn't all around them, like the forest and its food and such," Reyna said. "But they have lots of metal."

"They do!" Kell said. "They dig deep into the earth and bring back its prizes. They have so much more than they need. Their mines are bottomless."

Wren nodded. "I suppose."

"And you have seen them?" Hask said.

Reyna and Wren glanced to one another. "Yes," they lied in unison.

The other twins smiled.

"For all our desert kin lack, they are more than capable of keeping the source of their wealth a secret. If we could capture just *one* of their mines… There are many, I assume."

"Oh yes," Wren said.

"Many," Reyna agreed.

"If we could capture just one, we could be certain to keep Boviss's needs met and our village protected for generations to come."

"But what about the Fennecs? They would still need food, and you'd have more than enough."

Kell sighed. "That is lamentable. But there is just no way around that."

"What if you let them hunt here? What if you traded?" Reyna said.

"Boviss respects only strength. He would know, and we would both suffer," Kell said.

"That's what they said in the desert. Do you *know* that? Has anyone tried?" she said.

"The risk is too great should we be found out. Now the mines. Could you tell us how to get there? If we knew *precisely* where one was, and we went there directly, we could certainly send enough warriors to seize it."

He unfurled a map inked on vellum. The forest and its surroundings were quite precisely drawn. Farther from the forest, the markings became more general. A vague region, encompassing three whole mountains, bore the label *The Lair of Boviss*. Only slightly more precise was the region labeled *Burrow*. Anything much farther south than the Fennec village was simply labeled *Desert*. And where they sat was simply labeled *Gall*.

Wren scratched his head. "It was dark," he said.

"Very dark. And we are new to this place. We couldn't show you the way on a map," Reyna said.

"We could lead you, maybe."

The Red malthropes looked to one another.

"It would take great care," one suggested.

"But, perhaps, if you took one of our stealthiest. And one of our best fairies," suggested the other. "Once one of ours has been shown the way and returned, he could mark the place for others."

"But wouldn't it be dangerous?" Reyna asked.

"Oh, yes. Very dangerous. But you would be rewarded. And you would secure this paradise for the Red malthrope kind," Kell said.

"A prize worth any price," Hask said.

"If it's worth any price, then what would you do for us?"

Hask and Kell laughed.

"Bargainers, eh? What would you have in return?" Kell said.

"We want help getting Mama," Wren said.

The lightheartedness dropped from the faces of their hosts.

"It cannot be done," Hask said.

"But you said any price," Reyna countered.

"We would gladly help you if she were taken by anyone else. But Boviss—I am sorry, children. Your mother is gone."

"None return from Boviss's lair," Kell said.

"You don't know Mama," Wren said.

"I am sorry. It cannot be done."

"Will you show us where to find Boviss then?" Reyna asked.

"We do not know. Boviss does not wish to be found, and we do not wish to anger him. So we have never sought him," Hask said.

"But we will do anything else you desire. We will give you a home here. You will be like a prince and a princess. From this day forward, you will know only luxury, only adulation. You will be second only to Boviss in our prayers and praise," Kell said. "Will you do this for us? Will you show us the way to a mine?"

Reyna and Wren looked to one another with a brief glance.

"Of course," they replied again.

"Splendid!" Kell said.

He set down the wrapped cloth treat and opened it for them. It was a pair of buns. They had a spicy-sweet scent that made the young malthropes' jaws tingle at a single whiff. They snatched up the confections and gobbled them down. Never had either tasted anything like them. The humans, the elves, they made treats that were delightfully sweet, but this… this was a dessert made for a malthrope's palate.

"Ha!" Hask said. "The surest way to a child's heart. Come! We shall find you a home to watch you for a few days. And when you have your strength, you shall become the heroes you were destined to be!"

#

After a tour that served to reinforce just how magnificent a place the village was, Wren and Reyna were taken to one of the larger homes. A plump female welcomed them. In all their lives, the pair had never imagined that any malthrope could live well enough to earn so hearty a physique. She spoke only a chattering language like the Fennecs. In fact, in all the village, only Hask and Kell seemed to speak so-called dragon language. She was nonetheless happy to have them, and after a second supper at her insistence, they were given a cozy, safe room all their own to sleep in.

When they were left alone with full bellies and eyes almost too heavy to keep open, they looked to one another.

"We can't stay," Wren said.

He spoke Tresson so as to avoid being understood, and his disappointment with the statement was abundantly clear.

"Of course we can't," Reyna said. "They won't help us find Mama, and nice as they seem, the way they plot against the Fennecs..."

"And the way the Fennecs plot against *them*..." Wren agreed.

"They're like anyone else. Like the humans or the elves or the dwarves or anyone. I'd hoped our kind would be better..."

"So what do we do?" Wren asked.

"You saw the map, right?" Reyna said.

"It doesn't help much," Wren said.

"But do you think you could find Boviss if you had to?"

"I could find *anyone*." His bravado wavered a bit. "But what do we do when we find him?"

"We'll figure something out. But we can't wait anymore. We have to go."

Wren nodded.

"Right." He leaned closer and whispered more quietly. "So what did you get?"

The tiniest grin curled her lips as she began to produce items from her robe. He did so as well. A respectable mound of useful things they'd harvested from their hosts during the tour of the village piled up between them. Another knife, some rope, three small canteens, a few bottles of what may have been liquor of some kind. It was a wonder they'd been able to carry it all without being noticed. Just another fine lesson well learned from their mother.

They split the goods up as evenly as they could, such that each would have proper equipment if they were to get separated. When they were through, Wren's eyes lingered on the soft bedding of what could have been their home.

"We can't sleep here. We need to leave as soon as we can," Reyna said.

"I know… Wherever Mama is, she isn't sleeping in a nice soft bed." He turned his eyes to the window, and the forest beyond. "Let's go."

Chapter 9

Sorrel tugged at the chain about her neck. No amount of probing at the restraint would do her any good. The blasted thing had no lock. Whatever magic had reduced the chain to a dozen yards or so in length had also fused the shackle without so much as a keyhole. In all, the mound of chain attached to her weighed about as much as she did. It was inconvenient, but not impossible to tote along by itself. But when she'd reached the portion of Boviss's lair with his mound of gold, he'd tipped the huge stone statue and pinned the end of her chain beneath it, leaving her with slack enough to investigate barely a quarter of the massive chamber.

And that was how her time since then had been spent. He would walk her around from time to time like a pet, showing her this piece of his hoard or that, to brag. She would eat of his scraps. He would stare at her from atop his mound of riches. Something in his eyes made her feel like little more than another of the prizes that were scattered about. She supposed that was all she was.

Though he saw through it, Sorrel made certain to shower him with praise every now and then. He may have known she was insincere, but there was no denying the glimmer in his eye as he heard her words lavished upon him.

"You have so much wealth. You lair is so enormous. Even someone of your size could not use it all. Perhaps you could find a place for me. A place to stow me for those times when you desire solitude."

"A place where you can plot your escape unobserved? No. You remain where I can see you." He shifted a bit, to get more comfortable atop his gold. "A malthrope from across the sea," he mused. "How does a creature such as you find her way from one shore to another? The malthropes of the villages in my domain show little interest in the ocean. And I cannot imagine a human, elf, or dwarf taking you as a passenger."

"I came in secret. In a box. They believed me a wild animal for a menagerie."

"Fitting that you found your way to just such a fate."

She shut her eyes and tried to keep the tremor of anger from surfacing. "A collection this grand? I could not dream of such a thing," she said, oozing admiration as authentically as she could manage. "You, who are so great."

"Feh. I get enough of that drivel from the others. Tell me. What has become of the land across the sea?"

"Two great kingdoms wage war."

"Oh? To what end?"

"Does it matter? Kingdoms don't seem to need a reason."

"Not so. There is always a reason. Or an excuse. But I wouldn't expect minds as small as yours to be curious of such things."

She narrowed her eyes briefly. "I may be small and rare. But you are grand and mighty. You must have stories to tell."

"You would have me entertain you?" he rumbled.

She spread her arms. "You surround yourself with trophies. Those below? They worship you for what you are. Here, I can worship you for what you've *done*. Tell me of your great deeds."

Boviss tipped his head. "And I imagine you suspect you will trick me into revealing secrets to you." He leaned closer to her. "You are not so clever as you may think."

She clutched her hands and lowered her head. "I only wish to know of your adventures, oh great Boviss, the one who protects my people."

He shook his head. "Pathetic. But the days are long, and there is little to fill them. So you will have your tales. You will have no use for what little lessons they teach you."

He raised his head and spread his wings. "Eyes such as yours may look upon my hoard and imagine that those things within this chamber are my greatest treasures. Such are the delusions of a small mind."

Boviss scooped up a clawful of gold nuggets from the mound that made up his bed and let them sprinkle down in a glittering rain. "The blood and sweat of your people brought me this. A trifling. Fit to sleep upon. I have more gold caught among my scales than your kind will see in a lifetime. My greatest achievement is the lair itself."

He drew in a deep breath, puffing up his chest and kindling a deep orange glow within his throat. He released a column of flame that lanced down the hallway on his left. The lights were illuminated, revealing its scope and splendor. Another breath curled over Sorrel's head, threatening to roast her alive. One after another, he belched flames down the remaining hallways until the grandness of his lair was made clear. This place was large enough to house a sprawling city. Not just something like the Fennecs called home. This could rival the towering places of wood and stone that the humans called home. Or the elves. Or…

"Dwarves," Boviss stated. "Even you can't have missed their marks all around you. Many once called this mountain home. They dig deep into the world, stabbing at its heart. But one dwarf led his people upward. With their picks and their machines, they sought to hollow the whole of the mountain, to make it into some hideous monument to their industry. They created something grander than they deserved."

He padded down from his bed of gold and ran a claw across the surface of one of the columns. The carving there depicted some massive battle, dwarf against dwarf. But slashed across the carving was something that spoke of a less glorious battle. Marks that matched Boviss's own claws gouged long furrows out of the stone.

"They are tenacious, the dwarves. The battles lasted for years. Their busy little minds dreamed up machines to battle me. I roasted them by the score. Trampled them beneath my feet. They forged those chains to bind me. Their wizards created weapons that might even have cleaved my scales if they'd had warriors mighty enough to reach me. They did not. But still they fought on."

He swept his tail down and hooked the chain that held Sorrel. The swift motion yanked her forward and sent her sprawling, but also pulled the other end free of where he'd pinned it and wrapped it about the tail's spiked end. It was a motion he'd mastered, one he performed every time he felt the need to drag her about like a dog on a leash.

"Follow…" he ordered, as though she had a choice.

#

A misting rain fell upon the edge of the forest as the twins rushed along. For better or worse, possibly because they saw them as their own kind rather than enemies, the Reds hadn't treated Wren or Reyna as prisoners. They'd slipped from the village without much effort, though now the wind from behind carried the subtle but persistent scent of pursuers.

"Maybe we should have waited until night," Wren murmured quietly as he and his sister plodded along the muck that the rain had made of the forest floor.

"No," Reyna said sluggishly. "Not a minute longer than we need to."

"If they catch us, we lose the day."

"Then we don't let them catch us."

Wren blinked the water from his eyes. "That means no hiding. They know the forest better than we do. And hiding doesn't take us any closer to Mama. We need to… *down*!"

He shoved Reyna into a pool of mud and plopped down beside her. They each drew a deep breath and wallowed deep into the thick goop. A few moments later, a glittering form buzzed through the air above them. A water fairy was tracking them like a hunter's hound. It lingered for a moment, then continued on.

The twins waited as long as they could before resurfacing and gasping softly for air.

"Mama never taught us anything about fairies," Reyna said.

"I guess maybe Mama doesn't know everything."

They drew themselves out of the mud and continued on. Sloppy, wet forest floor made for slow going. It also meant the path behind was difficult to conceal. But the slow going cut both ways. Even if they found the traces of the path the twins traveled, those seeking them wouldn't be able to move much faster than the young ones could.

The day dragged on, and the drizzle turned into a downpour. This pitched things further in favor of Reyna and Wren, as the pounding drops drowned out any sort of sound the twins might make, tamped down the scent, and wiped away some of the trace they left behind. But too much travel and too little sleep were taking their toll on the twins. Worse, they didn't have much choice when it came to which way to go. They were heading for the mountains. They didn't know precisely where Boviss could be found, but the map they'd been shown narrowed it down to a cluster of three mountains northeast of the village. They had to move in that direction, or they'd be wasting precious time. But as they drew nearer, the wind blew down from the mountains more and more. That wind would carry their scent back to their trackers.

A few hours more sapped them of enough strength to make them sloppy. They'd stumbled upon an old riverbed that was beginning to flow again thanks to the downpour. The smooth stones in and around the crystal-clear water meant they could move at a near run without leaving prints or fouling their steps. It was the perfect place to move without a trace. And if Sorrel had seen them dashing along it, she would have pounced upon them and scolded them. The perfect place to escape a hunter is the first place a hunter would look.

"How…" Reyna swallowed hard. "How much farther to the mountains…"

"I don't know. There's not even a slope. It must be a long way."

She wiped her eyes. The constant rain had washed most of the mud from her face, but it was also terribly cold. Coupled with their tramping along in the reawakened stream, she was shivering. She paused to try to will away the quaking in her bones. Wren made it a few strides more before he noticed she'd faltered.

"Reyna. Just a little farther. If we… *Reyna!*"

The same pounding rain that made their motions as good as silent to their trackers did the same for the buzz of little wings. Some combination of good luck and better intuition had allowed them to hide whenever the fairies had approached before. But their luck had run out. A glimmering form was flitting directly toward them.

Wren grabbed Reyna's arm and hauled her forward as fast as he could. It was a heroic act, but he was as tired and cold as she was, and he managed to coax only a few extra strides out of her before he lost his footing and both of them splashed down into the water.

They floundered. The rush of water caught them, and the pair was washed down the stream. Reyna coughed and sputtered, trying to paddle for the shore. Layers of clothes and heaps of stolen goods were excellent for surviving when on the run in the woods. When caught in the current of a flash flood, they were very nearly a death sentence. Their weight dragged her below the surface. Her blurry vision caught first a glimpse of the thrashing form of her brother, then the wavering glow of the fairy who had spotted them. The glow vanished. Wren and Reyna bounced and tumbled along the river bottom. Stones clattered and rattled beneath them. Something solid struck Wren. He blindly wrapped an arm around it and flailed for his sister. She missed his paw, but caught his tail.

Neither knew quite what it was that had served as a sudden and painful anchor, but they didn't care. They scrambled along it and, with a few grateful and heaving breaths, flopped onto the rain-drenched shore.

Reyna coughed and sputtered. She blinked rain and mud from her eyes to find her brother still clutching a stout vine that had emerged from the ground. Reyna couldn't remember passing it, and she was quite certain it would have stuck out to her, as it was the vivid, brilliant green of new growth.

Wren hauled himself up onto his elbows and glared at the tiny figure perched atop the vine. He coughed. "Losh?"

The fairy teetered a bit and flopped forward. Wren caught him.

"Losh… make vine." He shook his head. "Not easy…"

"Why are you here?" Reyna asked. "H-how did you find us?"

"Reyna, Wren, Losh. Friends. Losh always find friends." He shook his head and flitted back into the air. "No one find Losh friends. Follow."

#

Sorrel huffed a breath and shuffled forward, led along by Boviss at the end of her chain. It hadn't taken much to get the dragon talking. He may not have been fooled by her words of praise, but the effect had been the same. After two unbroken hours of constant boasting, he'd not even finished listing off the achievements in the central part of his lair.

"And here," he rumbled, leaning low to a lance embedded in the stone. "Handled by five dwarves. The nearest any came to piercing my hide. And still it was scarcely a scratch."

He raised his wing and curled his neck to glance at the scar left by the attack. It was quite low along his side. As large as Boviss was, any wound in a battle against lesser creatures couldn't hope to reach higher than the thickest plates of his armored underbelly. It was certainly deeper than the mere scratches that showed on this plate of armor or that, but it was still superficial. Far from the weak spot she would have hoped his boasts would eventually uncover. It underscored just how mighty he truly was.

"You are strong," Sorrel said, reaching up toward the mark.

"Invincible," Boviss corrected. "The mere mention of my name is enough to keep the elves in the south where they belong. No human, no dwarf, no creature great or small will challenge me. The whole of North Crescent trembles in fear that my shadow might cross their lands. I chased the dwarves from their greatest city. Do you have any notion how viciously they defend what is theirs? But they are gone, never to return. What was theirs is mine."

"And yet you need our people to feed you. To supply you with fresh wealth."

He threw his head back. The lair trembled with his laughter.

"Do you believe that I *need* your kind?"

He strutted toward what remained of the offering of food. Much of it remained uneaten, and from the looks of the nearby mounds of bones and sinew, a dozen or more such offerings had been left untouched. The coolness and dryness of the cave kept them from rotting, but they were nonetheless rendered inedible piles of wasted flesh.

"Look at this. Simple tastes for simple creatures. An easy meal, but my proper meals come from the sea."

"But… if you do not need the food, and you do not need the wealth…"

"Oh, I do enjoy the gold." He stirred the mound idly. "More is always better than less."

"But the food."

He padded back to his precious mound of gold and curled atop it. "What can you make of that riddle, I wonder?"

"You have nothing to prove. You know you are mighty. We know you are mighty."

"Mmm," he murmured in vague agreement.

"… Then why?" Sorrel said. "Why make demands of my people. Is it cruelty?"

Boviss rolled to his back, sweeping his tail. The motion whipped her off her feet. "Cruelty. You say you are rare in the place you call home. Here, there are many. Your people live because of me. You would call that cruelty?"

She stood and wrestled away a tremor of anger. "Then why demand so much?!"

"Because it is not charity either."

"Then request less. Request food from the forest and wealth from the desert. I have been among those of the desert. What you do now pits desert against forest."

Boviss shook with a deep chuckle. Sorrel's jaw tightened.

"That is why you do this…" she fumed.

"My years are many, Child of the Forest Across the Sea. One must fill one's time. Battling endless hoards of tiny, worthless things is wearying. So we find other ways. We let them battle one another. We tug their strings. We watch the show."

He raised his tail. The chain drew tight, lifting Sorrel into the air by her neck. She grasped the chain to keep from being strangled as he lifted her over his grinning maw.

"The gifts of food and gold are how your kind show your gratitude to me. And you may think I have no gratitude for *you*. Untrue. You have brought me much entertainment. And for that I am quite grateful."

He flicked his tail. Sorrel swung aside and slid to a stop on the floor.

"Silence now. And sleep. Tomorrow I shall show you more of what I have gathered in my years. And when I am through?" He lowered his head and shut his eyes. "I am certain I can find some way to wring more entertainment out of you."

He settled comfortably down onto his golden bed and slipped into the effortless sleep of a creature with nothing to fear. Sorrel shakily climbed to her feet and dusted herself off. Her chain was still tangled with the massive dragon's tail. She wouldn't be escaping anytime soon. A bit of tugging and hauling got her near enough to the wasted mounds of food to snatch a bit of the fresh offering to eat. As she gnawed at the meal, she gazed at the sleeping dragon. The lights overhead faded slowly, drained of their stolen magic.

This… was life. She could survive this. Like everything else she had faced, she could survive it. There was food. And as wise as the creature believed itself to be, it was not beyond her skills of manipulation. This would not be pleasant, but it would be life. At least until he grew weary of her. There was no telling how long that would be.

Her eyes drifted to the faint glow of her mystic chain.

She would simply have to ensure the time she had was long enough.

#

Far below, many hours later, the twins were curled against one another, huddled into the crook of a branch far above the ground and deep asleep. They'd kept moving for as long as they could, but even a young malthrope couldn't run forever without sleep. Losh sat atop them, eyes fixed on the forest below. He'd done the work already, coaxed the wind into an obliging coil. It wouldn't carry the scent of the young ones away. The Reds from the village had come and gone. They had no reason to believe the twins might have the aid of a fairy, and so they trusted that if their scent was absent, so too were their targets. Now there was nothing to do but sit and wait.

The rain pattered to a stop in time for the last of the sun's rays to offer a bit of warmth before the coolness of night set in. By rights, the little ones could have—and should have—slept through the whole of the night and well into the day. They'd spent the last night in search of the village of the Red malthropes. Their respite within its borders was brief. Alas, raw exhaustion couldn't wipe from their minds the important task at hand. They'd been running for a reason, and that reason haunted their dreams just as surely as it haunted their waking hours.

Reyna was the first to stir. She pulled herself groggily upright. Her sleep-dulled senses caused her to teeter a bit until she remembered, with a jolt of fear, that she was two dozen feet off the ground on a branch.

"Reyna awake," Losh said. "No forest children. Losh hide Reyna."

She nodded numbly. "Thank you, Losh. You are a good friend."

"Best friend!" Losh crowed.

Reyna nudged her brother awake. After a similar startled jump nearly sent him tumbling from the branch, he shook away the shreds of sleep and pieced the world back together with an unwilling and still quite weary mind. One piece didn't want to fall into place.

"You're still here," he said thickly, eyes on the fairy.

"Best friend," the fairy said sternly, as though irritated he'd not been listening.

"But why?" Reyna asked. "All we did was give you some of that stuff. And we don't even have any more."

Losh opened his little mouth, but he paused. The scattering of words he knew clearly wasn't enough to articulate his thoughts on the matter.

"Reyna, Wren. Forest children. Burrow. Place of desert children. Desert children say forest children bad. Reyna, Wren, could be bad." He swiped his hand. "Not bad. Reyna, Wren, could ask for bad from Losh. Not ask for bad. Reyna, Wren, could do bad *to* Losh. Not do bad. Reyna, Wren good."

He pointed. "Forest children? Big place of forest children? Bad. Reyna, Wren good. Forest children bad. Losh do good, so good forest children know good is better than bad."

"You're rewarding us for not being as bad as the Fennecs said we would be?"

"Reward! Also thank. Reward and thank." Losh considered his next words. "And Losh not go far until Reyna and Wren. Reyna and Wren, good reason for go far. Losh stay. Losh help. Best friend."

Reyna grinned. "It's good to have a friend. I… I don't think we've ever had one. And now that you're here, you can keep us from ever being found."

Losh shook his head. "Desert children find Losh someday. Fairies find fairies. If forest children look for fairy, forest children find. Forest children no look for fairy. Desert children look for fairy."

"Oh… That could be a problem," Reyna said.

Losh nodded. Wren shook his head.

"No, it won't be a problem. It doesn't matter if they can find us or not." He held tight to the trunk of the tree and leaned aside to look to the northeast. "Because pretty soon, we'll be somewhere they wouldn't dare follow."

Reyna took a breath. "That's right, Losh. You might not be so happy to be friends with us when we tell you where we are going."

"We're going to find Boviss," Wren said.

Losh blinked at them. "Find Boviss. And? Why bad for Losh?"

Reyna raised her eyebrows. "You're not afraid of Boviss?"

"Why Losh afraid? Fairies very small. Dragon very big. Dragon not care about fairies. Dragon scare bigger things that scare fairies. Dragon *good* for fairies. Friend of fairies." He flitted closer as if to whisper a secret. "Not *best* friend. But friend. Not bad for Losh."

Reyna smiled. "I'm glad you're not afraid of him."

"That makes one of us."

"Reyna and Wren scared? Why go?"

"Because of Mama," Wren said.

Losh considered this. "Good reason. Best reason, maybe."

"Do you know how to find Boviss's lair?" Reyna asked.

Losh shook his head.

"I can find it," Wren said.

"You're sure? We don't know what a dragon smells like," Reyna said.

Wren crossed his arms. "'Swift and the Special Fruit.'"

Losh flitted up between their faces. "What that?" he asked.

"A story Mama tells," Reyna said.

"And in that story, Swift is challenged to find a special fruit. It is *so* special that no one has ever seen it, tasted it, or even smelled it. They knew it was somewhere in the woods because… of a wizard or something. But Swift found it because he knew everyone else was looking for it, and they'd not come close enough to smell it or see it. So even though he didn't know where to find it, he knew he would be close when he found a place where he didn't smell anyone else. If no one had been there, then it *must* have been close to the fruit. Then he sniffed for a smell he'd never found before. What lesson did we learn, Reyna?"

"You can find a thing if you know all of the places it isn't," Reyna said. "But this isn't like that! We *don't* know all of the places Boviss isn't."

"Is Boviss scary?" Wren asked.

"Very," Reyna said.

"Not scary for fairy," Losh corrected.

"Why is he scary? Because he's a hunter, and we're all prey to him, that's why. And what does good prey do when a hunter is nearby?"

"It stays away," Reyna said, realization dawning.

"We're hunting a hunter, so we have to hunt *backward*. We go where the prey isn't, and that's where the hunter is."

"We've never done something like that," Reyna said. "Are you sure you can do it?"

Wren looked at her steadily, no hint of doubt in his eyes. "I know I can."

"And what do we do when we get there?"

He shrugged and dug his claws into the tree, ready to climb down. "That's your part. I'll find him. You figure out how to beat him."

"Why do I have the hard job?!" she retorted.

"It's not *my* fault you're the smart one. Now let's go."

Chapter 10

Sorrel had learned, much to her chagrin, that while Boviss was a sound sleeper, he was not a still sleeper. He rolled over, sometimes quite suddenly, every few hours. Worse, his tail would sweep and swing as he slept. Aside from the endless cascade of gold that clattered and kept her awake, it wasn't so much of a problem. But today, she was chained to his tail. If she stayed clear of the sweep of the tail, there wasn't enough slack on the chain and she would be heaved aside during the sweeps. So she was forced to remain at the fringe of this mound of gold and watch the motions of the tail like a hawk lest he smash her to paste while he slept. It was a harrowing, exhausting experience… but perhaps fate had been kind in subjecting her to it.

In his boasting, Boviss had claimed there was more gold trapped between his scales than most creatures would ever see. It was quite so. But there were other things trapped there as well. Years of battle may have turned away the blades of thousands of attackers, but some bit deeper than perhaps even *he* knew. As Sorrel peered in the darkness, she saw something embedded deep between two scales near the tip of his tail. It wasn't gold or silver. The metal was too dull. When the hazardous limb swept toward her and splashed a scattering of gold at her, she risked inching closer. She'd become quite accustomed to the gloom of the lair when the lights overhead darkened. The very chain that bound her, for all its problems, glowed enough to give shape to her surroundings. And in its glow, she saw that the thing embedded in the tail was a stout, broad arrowhead. If it had bitten deep enough into his tail to remain there for however many years it had, it must have been of supernatural construction.

The tail swept away. To protect her hand, she wrapped as much of her tattered clothing around it as she could, and waited. When the tail swept back, she grasped the broken shaft and pulled with all her strength. He started to sweep his tail away again. It dragged her along a bit before the arrowhead finally popped free. Sorrel spilled onto the gold and had to roll desperately aside to avoid being crushed as the tail flopped back down. Her heart hammered in her chest, but not because she'd nearly been killed. This was it. She might have a chance to escape her bonds.

She turned the arrowhead over in her hands. It was definitely a piece of dwarven enchantment. Sorrel hated magic of any sort. That hatred had only grown in the days she'd been kept here by the blasted enchantment on her restraints. But she knew full well that most times the only way to beat magic was with more magic. Something here would be able to cut the chain. She just had to find it. The problem was that he was never foolish enough to give her even a moment without his watchful gaze while she was near enough to reach the weapons. Even if he left his back turned long enough for her to grab one, none was small enough to hide until she could put it to use. But now she had one, and it was small enough to hide.

Sorrel huddled down and split her attention between dodging the tail and working at the chain. She dragged the little arrowhead in slow, firm strokes across a chain link near her neck. She used the utmost of care, not just to keep the motions as silent as she could manage, but to ensure the scraping of the tool always found the same spot. After what seemed like ages, she gave her near-numb fingers a break and ran a claw along the link. Her claw clicked against an insignificant little groove that she was certain wasn't there before. It was tiny, but it wasn't nothing. This would work. All it would take was time and care.

She'd done more with less.

#

Reyna, Wren, and Losh's travels had taken them quite far. After a few hours of fumbling and stumbling, Wren had gotten the knack of ignoring his instincts and seeking out the places where nothing worth hunting could be found. Since then, they'd been moving steadily northward. Their journey had taken them into the night and out again. The sky was rosy with dawn.

Whoever had made the map that Hask and Kell had shown them had been on the right track. It would seem the northernmost of the three mountains labeled as Boviss's lair was the place the beast truly called home.

Each step forward filled the twins with a bit more anxiety, but not always the anxiety that seemed proper.

"Wren?" Reyna said, after her thoughts had stewed for as long as she could stand.

He grunted in reply, unwilling to take his nose from the task.

"Did you think it would be this way?"

He glanced over his shoulder with a questioning look.

"Other malthropes. Did you ever think about what it would be like if we found some?"

"All the time," he said. "I didn't ever think it would happen, though."

"I did. I always did. Everyone else has a place. Why wouldn't we have a place? But I didn't expect this. I didn't expect the first malthropes we found to lock us up and tear us apart. I didn't expect them to fight each other."

"Maybe it's a good thing." Wren raised his head to trace his eyes up along the stark gray of the mountain. "The climbing will get harder from here on."

"How could it be a good thing?"

"It means we're not so different. It's the same thing all the other creatures do. Maybe it means we're the same."

"I don't *want* to be the same if that's what it means," Reyna said.

"Flower!" Losh blurted and darted toward a cluster of ice-blue blooms clinging to the face of the mountain so he could drink the flowers' nectar.

They scampered up to a ledge and surveyed their surroundings. The mountains were rising out of the forest now. They were far enough from the Gall that they no longer had to worry much about hiding, and there wasn't much sense trying to hide if Boviss showed up. They were trying to find him, and there would be no getting away from him besides. It was liberating to stand tall again, unafraid of being pursued for the time being.

From this vantage, they could see over the tops of the trees. The sun peeked up over the mountains, pouring its golden light over the landscape below.

"Look at it..." Wren murmured, eyes taking in the glorious view. "It's all here. You can *see* it all from here. Forest. Desert. I see snow, up to the north. This is it. This is the world. Anything you might want, right here. And our people, too. This is what we were looking for. We crossed an ocean. We journeyed up from the south. This is it. This is the place."

"And it's filled with the same stuff we were running from. Plus a big dragon," Reyna said.

Wren stared at the land. "Of course it is. Because we have to earn it."

"Earn it?"

"Do we get a meal just for finding a deer? No. We have to chase it. We have to corner it. We have to wrestle it to the ground. We have to *earn* it." He stood. "This place is perfect. It's everything we want. We found it. Now we have to earn it." He turned to her. "The bigger the prize, the bigger the fight. And this is the biggest prize of them all. It's worth it, isn't it?"

She nodded and stood beside him. "It is. It really is. All of it. The place. The people. If we want this to be our home, if we want to stop searching and stop running, we're going to have to fight all these fights. We're going to have to get the Reds and the Fennecs to stop their fighting. We're going to have to do something about Boviss. We're going to have to do it all." She gave him a sideways glance. "Are you *sure* I'm the smart one?"

Wren sampled the breeze. "You better be the smart one. Because if that smell isn't Boviss, I don't know what is. And I sure don't know what we're going to do about him yet."

He shielded his eyes. "We've got half a mountain to climb. You've got until then to come up with a plan that would make Swift proud."

Reyna spotted the shadow-shrouded peak that Wren had set his eyes upon. "I'll think of something," she said with a resolute gleam in her eye.

#

Sorrel's time with Boviss had been unpleasant, but not intolerable. Even eating just the crumbs off his plate, she was better fed as his personal pet than she'd been for years on her own. He had little regard for her safety, constantly flailing her about whenever he had her hooked to his tail, but she was quick to learn his whims and anticipate when she'd have to brace herself. There were only two things about this place that had been truly trying.

The first was the knowledge that somewhere out there her children were forced to do without her. She'd taught them as well as she could, but this was a strange new place with things she'd never anticipated. She didn't know what had become of them, and she would not have a proper moment of sleep until she saw their faces again.

Her other source of difficulty was a sad necessity. In her desire to keep Boviss from having a taste of her, Sorrel had awakened a taste for her praise in *him*. And like so many other things in his life, Boviss was not content until he had overindulged himself.

"Have you lost your tongue, Child of the Forest Across the Sea?" Boviss rumbled.

He, and thus she, had taken their place at the mouth of his lair. He gazed over a vista that encompassed half the continent. As he did, he enjoyed the adulation that Sorrel had become quite adept at delivering despite the lack of sincerity.

"It is simply that you have taken my breath away. That is all," Sorrel said. "You, who are so great. I have never seen a dragon so great as you."

"Certainly not. A beast that can become an elder dragon is born but once in a generation. And that is a *dragon's* generation. The world may only have seen three of my kind since it was born. Before me, there was my mother."

"And her mother before her?" Sorrel suggested.

"No. Before her was a creature from what you have called Tressor. A place where humans and dragons have linked their fates."

"The place of Dragon Riders. I have heard of this place."

"Many thousands of years ago. Many, *many* thousands of years ago, there was an elder dragon there. She was the largest. The oldest. Our legends say she was hatched of the world itself, that it was her fires that boiled away enough of the sea for the creatures of land to take their places. And she fell to my mother. And my mother fell to me."

"You killed your own mother?" Sorrel said.

"There is room for only one elder. Had I not killed her, she would have killed me. And I would have deserved it for not rising to the challenge," he said.

"I suppose it must have been trickery, oh great Boviss."

"Trickery…" he fumed. "Do you believe I could not conquer her with my might alone?"

"Surely a battle with one of your size would have churned the mountains to gravel."

"Such flowery language. Even you could not believe that."

"Then the battle was a swift one? Your mother was feeble?"

He rumbled with a tremor of anger. "Have you grown weary of your time here? Are you longing for the escape of death? My mother was every bit as mighty as I. My skill with my claws and my flame, and my cunning, brought me the victory that day, and only after a struggle that lasted weeks."

"But you show no scratch. No scar of that day. How could such a battle be one without a wound?"

"That day, I was as near as this world is ever likely to bring me to death," he said. He held his foreleg toward her. "Look upon me. If you do not see the scar of that day, then your vision has failed you."

She peered at the offered leg. It was subtle, but it was there. The untold centuries since the battle had faded the scar and hidden it between rows of healthy scales, but a deep white split some of his armor.

"I see. Truly the battle must have been one for the ages."

"It is a battle the likes of which this world will never see again."

"Oh? What, then, of your own young? Won't they rise to challenge you?"

"There shall be no young. I shall reign as elder for as many days as this world has left." He turned to her. "You see, now, how wise your kind have been to choose me as their patron."

"And you, who are so great, who are so mighty and can never be vanquished, why limit your land only to what you see here? Why should your domain have borders?"

"My land *has* no borders. The world is my domain."

"I can tell you that the people of Tressor, and of the northern places, do not think this is so. No one utters your name there. Not in praise and not in fear."

"That proves only ignorance. Something this world has in abundance." He shook the chain from his tail and snagged it instead with his claw. "The offerings of your people have left me wanting," he muttered. "It is time for a proper meal."

He paced inside. Sorrel dashed at a near-sprint to avoid being dragged. He tipped back the much-abused statue that had become something of the official stake for her chain.

Boviss didn't bother offering his flame to the hanging lights above. He simply left her in the darkness, tethered to a statue she couldn't hope to lift. She watched him go, and when she was certain he would not return, she produced the arrowhead from its hiding place and put it back to work, just as she had for each precious moment free of his gaze.

The arrowhead was fashioned by dwarves to wound a dragon, so it was every bit strong enough to peck at the chain. But the chain was designed for a dragon as well, and it put up quite a fight. She persevered. Slow progress had rewarded her with an ever-widening gap. The first half of the link had been shaved away to nearly nothing. She'd lost track of just how long it had taken to get this far, and it was still only half the job of breaking the chain link and setting her free, but as the last few slivers of metal scraped away, she could feel her pulse quickening.

A final scratch broke through the link. Etchings and runes that had been softly glowing since the chain had latched on to her flared suddenly brighter. In the light they cast, she saw the damaged chain link peel open. It dropped away and faded to darkness. For a brief, glorious moment she had only a short length of chain hanging from her neck, and she was free of the heavy statue that anchored her. Then the loose links of chain popped open and drew themselves together. They joined with an arcane flash. Just like that, the chain was strong as ever. All she'd managed to do was make it a link shorter.

Sorrel trembled with fury. She spat profanities in every language she knew. A vicious throw sent the broken chain link clattering down the hallway leading back to the outside world. She screamed until her lungs ached. Silence only came when a deep breath revealed something that stirred even more potent emotions.

She turned to the hallway and drew in another breath. The faintest breeze from the outside carried the scent of lost freedom, and now, two more familiar scents. In the near darkness, it was difficult to see what, if anything, was coming. But she didn't need to see it. She could smell it. She could hear it. And even if those senses were denied her, she could *feel* it.

Her young ones were coming.

They scampered along with the near-silent padding of their feet that she'd spent their entire lives trying to silence further. Raw, potent emotions rushed through her as they drew nearer. She felt pride that they had come this far, fear that they might be caught if Boviss returned. There was relief, hope, and disappointment. But more than anything else, there was joy.

When they were finally near enough that a fresh whiff of her own scent reached their noses, the twins abandoned stealth and rushed toward her.

"Mama! Mama!" Reyna cried, bounding toward her on all fours.

"We found you!" Wren crowed, keeping pace with his sister.

The two young ones tackled their mother in a pair of hugs that threatened to squeeze the breath from her lungs.

"I knew we'd find you. I knew you'd still be alive," Wren said.

Sorrel held them tight and murmured sweetly and soothingly into their ears until they started to calm down. When the rush of seeing their mother again had passed, she gently pulled herself from the embrace and looked upon them. In the near darkness, only the sparkle of their tearful eyes betrayed them.

"My clever little ones," she said softly. "You aren't hurt, are you?"

"No, Mama!" they said.

"You are well-fed? You are strong? You are thinking clear and fast?"

"Yes, Mama!"

Sorrel nodded.

"Good." She gave both her twins a light bop on the back of the head. "Then why did you come to this place?!"

"We had to rescue you, Mama," Wren said.

"It isn't your job to keep me safe. It is my job to keep *you* safe. You should not have come here. I taught you better than that."

"But we waited until the dragon was gone."

"And we have a friend at the mouth of the cave watching for him," Reyna said.

"Our friend doesn't like caves," Wren explained.

"How do you have a friend?" she said dubiously.

"He's a *fairy*," Reyna said. "And we were nice to him and gave him food, and he's nice to us in return."

"You are *not* nice to him, because you brought him to a dragon's cave."

"But the dragon is *gone*, Mama! It was still flying away when we got to the cave," Wren said.

"Over the ocean. It was going *far*. It won't be back anytime soon," Reyna added.

"It has a nose, doesn't it? It will smell that you have been here. And there is nowhere it cannot get to. You should not have come here."

"But we did come here, Mama," Wren said.

"And if we stay or go, it will chase us just the same," Reyna said.

"So we might as well save you," Wren said.

Sorrel smirked. "Clever little ones. Fine. You have until we get a whiff of the dragon. Then, whether I am free or not, you go. You find a place to hide and you—"

"We won't need it, Mama!" Wren said. "You have a chain on you. Is that all?" He started to haul the chain through his paws, searching for its end.

"Is there a key?" Reyna asked.

"Can we break it?" Wren added.

"It is magic. No key, and if you break it, it fixes itself."

Wren reached the end of the chain and gazed up at the statue just barely discernible in its dim glow. "This is big…"

He tugged at the chain. Reyna joined him. Sorrel, though she knew all too well they wouldn't have a chance of budging it, hauled at the chain as well.

"What do we do? Reyna, it's your turn!" Wren said. "I found her like I said I would. Now you have to figure out how to get her free."

"I thought I was going to be figuring out how to defeat a dragon, not free Mama from chains."

"Enough!" Sorrel snapped. "Arguing doesn't help anything. I'll tell you what we need to do…"

"We need to break the statue!" Reyna said.

"We can't break the statue. Look how big it is!" Wren said.

"No, your sister is right. Other places, we could not, but there is much magic here. Many magic things. I cannot get them, because of the chain. But you can. Go! That way. Find things for breaking stone. This is a dwarf place. There will be things for breaking stone. And there will be tunnels too small for a dragon. Find one. A deep one. We'll need somewhere to hide because we'll never get far enough away to escape him before he returns."

"Yes, Mama!"

Chapter 11

The twins rushed through the darkness. Everything about this place was spine-tingling. Though they could barely see, the scope of the lair was still evident in the echo of their motions and the airy breaths of wind. It was as though the lair was its own little world, cut off from the outside. Every inch of the place was saturated with the scent of the dragon. Tracking Boviss was the first time they'd ever sampled such a scent, but a deep, instinctive fear shook them with every breath of his aroma. For such sensitive noses trained for survival, the smell was a treatise on things that they should avoid. He was ancient. He was enormous. He was well-fed. And this was his home.

It might have been more of a battle than they could bear, silencing the wise voices of antiquity who screamed at them to run from this place, but for two very important things. First, if they ran now, there was no telling what would happen to their mother. Second, the hallways surrounding them were filled with wonders enough to distract even the most terrified mind with their splendor.

"Look at this one," Wren breathed, dragging a silver-headed hammer out of a mound of equipment. It was all he could do to heft it from the ground.

"You need to be able to swing it, Wren," Reyna snapped. She raised her nose and sniffed the air.

"I could swing it once or twice. A hammer this big, I bet it could turn that statue to pebbles in two blows."

Reyna scrabbled up on a pile and sniffed again. "There's something this way, I'm sure of it."

"Here!" Wren said.

He pulled a fierce-looking weapon from the mound. If it were a bit cruder, one might have called it a pick ax. But like so many other things here, it was covered with spiderweb-thin etchings. Dust layered it, but a quick swipe of his thumb revealed a gleaming polished finish. And while one end of it had the blunt shape of something meant to cleave stone, the other side was a spike that could pierce through the heaviest of shields.

The weapon-cum-tool was still a bit heavy for Wren, but with a bit of teetering and balancing, he found he could wield it quite ably. A single blow to the wall fractured it.

"That'll do it, I'm sure of it!" Reyna said. "Go back to Mama and get to work."

"You aren't coming?"

"I've got to find a way out of here."

He nodded and bounded away as quickly as the heavy tool would allow. Reyna continued to stalk through the towering hallway. It was a bit of a trick she'd learned from Wren on the way to this place, but she had a feeling if she headed *away* from the smell of fresh, clean wind, she should find a place that led deeper into the mountain.

She moved with agonizing slowness, sampling the air a dozen times with each step. Just a hint of dankness. Just a dash of mustiness. And then something else… char.

Reyna crept toward the smell. This was the lair of a dragon. She would have imagined that char would be everywhere. Such hadn't been the case. True, there was no shortage of acrid, roasted scents. But a good long burn in a single place had a distinct aroma that was lacking everywhere else but in this corner of the hallway.

She found the source, a stretch of wall seared black, so baked by flame that the carvings had bubbled and crackled. The damaged patch of wall peeked out from behind a huge pile of twisted, gnarled armor. Each piece was small enough to move, but the pile as a whole was enormous.

"The dragon did this," Reyna murmured. "He tried to burn this wall, and then he tried to bury it. And I smell something else. Something behind it. There is a way out. There *must* be."

She rubbed her paws together and scrambled to the top of the pile to start throwing bits of armor aside.

#

Sorrel sat with her eyes shut. A malthrope lived and died by its senses. There were few races walking the world who had been more thoroughly gifted in terms of sight, sound, and smell. Unfortunately, there were always limits. Somewhere, Boviss was out there. Perhaps he was half an ocean away, hauling up a squirming leviathan, something fit to feed so massive a predator. But he might be just a few miles away, soaring back to find Sorrel and her children and char them to cinders. Every moment of warning was precious, so she did what she'd done a thousand times before. She shut out every sense but the one she used. She poured as much of her mind and soul as she could into wringing just that much more out of what her ears told her. It was as near to magic as she ever came.

She heard her little ones. The staggered padding of her boy toting something heavy. The rattling and rummaging of her girl. She could hear the flick of fairy wings. Wind curled about the peaks of the mountains outside. Far, far away she could hear the rustle of leaves. And farther still, not just at the edge of hearing, but at the edge of what she *imagined* she could hear, the leathery whistle of titanic wings tearing through the air. It simply wasn't possible that she truly heard Boviss, but all the same, she knew she was right.

"He's coming…" she murmured.

Wren skidded to a stop beside the mound of gold, pick in paw.

"We don't have much time," she said.

"Leave it to me, Mama," Wren said.

She gathered up the slack on her chain and tugged at it. Wren raised the pick and brought it down. The blunt head turned a fist-size piece of the towering statue into powder. Again and again he attacked the base of the statue. The dwarves truly knew how to make a tool. The statue crumbled as easily as a block of ice, but Boviss had taken care to set the chain deep beneath.

For a few minutes, Sorrel and Wren took turns tugging the slack out of the chain and swinging the pick. The base of the statue was nibbled away, turned bit by bit into powder and gravel. Soon the once grand statue was standing on a precariously thin base, but it had yet to free the chain.

Both mother and son were terribly winded from the effort, and though it probably wouldn't take more than another session or two from each of them to whittle the base of the statue away to nothing, it was clear that getting close enough to deliver the final few blows was a good way to end up crushed should it choose that moment to collapse.

Wren huffed and puffed, then gazed up.

"What are you thinking…" Sorrel asked uneasily.

"Be ready to run, Mama. I think this will work."

Before she could stop him, Wren shouldered the pick and scampered up along the body of the battered statue. The great figure had one hand held aloft, and the other supported a massive stone shield. The artists must have worked for ages to ensure that the weight of one balanced the other, and their work showed in the fact that the base had been chipped to barely a third of its original size and the statue had yet to tip. But Wren was going to change that. He dropped down from the head onto the outstretched arm, then slid down to the shoulder.

"Wren, you be careful!" Sorrel shouted.

"Just be ready to run!" Wren called back.

He put the pick to work. Chips of stone rained down. Sorrel stretched the chain to its limit and watched through half-squinted eyes. She didn't have to watch for long. After a dozen blows, the triumphantly raised arm split away. It landed with an ear-splitting smash. Without it to act as a counterbalance, the statue started to tip. Wren tipped along with it.

Sorrel's eyes widened. In the dimness of the cave it was difficult to see precisely where the motion of the tipping statue was taking it. The chain slipped free suddenly. Sorrel fell backward and scrambled away.

"Wren!" she cried.

She swept her eyes desperately over the teetering form, but she couldn't see if Wren had jumped free. When it finally landed, the statue came down directly atop the dragon's bed of gold. Perhaps it was something in the statue itself, or perhaps it was something hidden within the mound, but as the mass of stone struck, light lanced up from the hoard and curled through the air. It illuminated a wave of glittering nuggets. They splashed into the air and caught the light from the awakening chandeliers overhead. For a few moments the whole of the cave suffered an extravagant golden hailstorm.

Sorrel scrambled to her feet and rushed the mound, flinching as walnut-sized lumps of gold thunked down on either side.

"Wren, you answer me right now, or you never get another story again!" she hissed.

She sniffed her way across the mound. It took her a few heart-stopping moments to find the proper place to dig, but when she did, she drove her arm down into the gold and found the wrist of her boy. She tugged and dug until his head surfaced. He took a deep breath and shook some jewels from his hair.

"Did I do it?" he asked.

Sorrel hugged his head to her chest. "What you did was a foolish thing that almost killed both of us," she raved, rocking him back and forth. "But you didn't kill us, and I'm free. So good boy."

"Mama! Wren!" Reyna called, sprinting out of the hallway. "What happened? Is everyone all right?"

Wren climbed out of the mound of gold and dusted a fortune off his shoulders.

"We are not hurt," Sorrel said. "Did you find a hiding place?"

"I found a door, but it's shut tight."

Wren tugged the pick out of the hoard. "Not for long," he said.

Sorrel looked to the hallway behind. She shuddered. "Boviss is close. I can feel it." She looked down at the mound of gold she was standing on. "Quickly. Fill your pockets."

"Mama, if the dragon is coming, shouldn't we run?" Wren said.

"Gold won't do us any good if we're dead," Reyna said.

"Yes. These are very wise things to say. Fill your pockets anyway. This dragon will know that the gold is missing, and it will make him mad." Her eyes flashed with petty vengeance. "Some creatures deserve to be mad."

The twins nodded and filled their pockets to bulging. Sorrel stuffed as much as she could into the meager outfit she wore. Then she scooped up the slack of the chain and coiled it to make it easier to tote along with her. She nodded to them.

"Lead the way," she urged.

#

The trio rushed toward the blackened stretch of wall. Along the way, they'd been harvesting some choice bits of equipment. They'd acquired quite a tidy haul of valuables. Sorrel topped off her outfit with a dwarf-made cloak and bag. The twins found some light armor. Sorrel and Reyna each picked up a well-made sword, and Wren kept his pick.

They reached the pile of twisted armor Reyna had been working at. While Wren and Sorrel had been chipping away at the statue, Reyna had cleared away most of the pile and unearthed a sturdy door.

The surrounding wall and floor had been blasted so intensely with dragon fire that it was little more than crackled black glass. The door, its hinges, and the doorjamb around it had survived with little more than a coating of soot.

"I don't know if it is magic, or if the dwarves are just really good at building doors," Reyna said. "But smell. There's definitely a passage back there, one that hasn't been opened in ages. And if he attacked the door, the dwarves must have gone through it. And if the door is still here, it means he couldn't get them after."

Like seemingly everything that was a product of dwarven ingenuity, the door was far more complex than it needed to be. Rather than a knob or some other handle to pull it open, the door had complex linkages bracing it shut, and intricate mechanisms to operate them. The central placement of one of the devices suggested it was more important than the rest. It consisted of a pair of scoops shaped to roughly resemble hands. When one moved down, the other moved up, like two sides of a balance.

Sorrel gritted her teeth. "I have heard of things like this. The dwarves and their riddles…"

"I tried moving the hands all around, but the door never opened."

"There is probably magic. There is too much magic in this place," Sorrel rumbled. "Clean the door. They put clues sometimes. When someone thinks they are clever, they like to give hints to mock you. They like to prove you aren't as clever as they are."

She and the twins grabbed scraps of fabric from the bits of armor and rubbed at the door. Soot settled into the fine lines of carvings, casting them in brilliant contrast. Sure enough, the etchings *did* seem to tell a story. At the far sides of the door, stout figures in worker's garb were shown mining. The tale told was much the same on each side. As the scene moved closer toward the central mechanism, the bounty of the earth was further refined or became ingots. Ingots were melted and poured. Not until they'd reached quite near the center did the scenes differ much at all. On the left, the items being drawn from the molds were hammers and other tools. On the right, they were axes and shields.

"There's writing all around it," Wren said. "Do you know this language, Mama?"

"No. The dwarves stay away from malthropes, and I don't care to search for them."

The Story of Sorrel

Reyna gazed at the images. "It has to be magic. If it wasn't magic, it would only matter where the hands were."

Sorrel nodded. "Yes. With magic, what is *in* the hands would matter." She shook the chain. "This needed my blood to work."

"Let's just try things," Wren said.

The three of them piled things into the hands. Nothing seemed to work. Time ticked by. Sorrel became more frantic. Before long, the twins understood why. The wind from the outside carried the scent of the dragon. He would be here any moment.

"Maybe I can break it," Wren said, brandishing his stolen pick.

"No. If you break the lock but not a door, the door never opens," Sorrel warned. "We need another way out."

She grew silent. Her eyes narrowed. Her ears pivoted. The twins looked up and turned to the source of the distraction. It was the soft buzz of tiny wings. A faintly glowing form buzzed toward them. In a smooth motion, Sorrel snatched it out of the air. Losh struggled in her grip, but she'd grabbed him so tightly that only the top of his head poked out from her fingers.

"Mama! That's Losh. That's our friend the fairy," Wren said.

Sorrel gazed down at her young, then brought the little thing to her snout. She took a deep whiff that fluttered the little creature's unruly hair.

"This one is your friend?" she said, eyes distrustful slits as she scrutinized the captured earth fairy.

"Yes! He helped us escape," Wren said.

Sorrel glared at the little thing. "He helped *me* to be captured…" She loosened her fingers, and Losh plopped to the ground.

"Is that true, Losh?" Wren asked.

"Losh do job. Do job good. Losh job stop forest children." The fairy pointed to Sorrel. "Forest children like her. Losh best friend now. Losh not capture again." He flicked and buzzed his crumpled wings back into shape and flitted from the ground.

"What are you doing in here?" Wren asked. "I thought you were afraid of caves."

"Dragon comes. Losh said Losh warn." He nodded firmly. "Losh do good job for best friend."

The mountain trembled. A roar that could shatter bone echoed through the halls. Boviss was certainly home.

"We've got to find another place to hide. We are out of time," Sorrel said.

"Wait!" Reyna said. She'd not stopped staring at the door, working at its riddle. "Maybe this isn't the end of the story," she said, pointing at the pile of tools on one side. "This is all stuff that makes other stuff. Ore makes metal, metal makes tools. Tools make… anything that needs to be made."

She pulled a leather belt from the mound of armor and hooked it over the hand. The hand lowered under its weight. The right hand remained high. When it reached a certain point, the left hand held still.

"You could be right, but we've got to solve the other side," Wren said. "What do *weapons* make?"

"War, death…" Reyna reasoned.

"How are we going to put war or death on a hand, Reyna?" he asked.

"No, no…" Reyna murmured.

Sorrel gazed over her shoulder. The hallway was rattling with the heavy strides of the dragon. There were seconds remaining.

"Faster!" Sorrel said.

"Blood!" Reyna said. "The magic needed blood. Weapons make blood."

She nipped the back of her finger and let a drop fall on the open palm. Though it was but a single drop, the hand began to slide down just as surely as the one weighed down by the belt.

All three of them tugged madly at the door as the dragon drew near enough for his furious breath to echo through the halls. When the hand reached its level, the door produced a soft click. The blood glowed brilliantly and vanished. Linkages shifted. Braces lifted. And just as the first curling flames lanced down the hallway toward them, the three malthropes and the fairy tumbled through the door.

Sorrel snatched the belt from its place and scrambled around to heave the door shut. As soon as it was closed, the linkages snapped and clicked to secure it.

Steep stone steps awaited them. For a moment, the way forward was illuminated only by Losh's glow. They rushed down the steps just in time for a new light to fill the room. Flame wreathed the door. They bounded to the nearest landing and turned to the doorway.

The Story of Sorrel

The dwarf-made door hissed and sizzled. Boviss roared in anger and belched flame at it until it glowed cherry-red. But it held firm. They were safe from him. For now.

Chapter 12

The malthrope family and their little friend made their way through what seemed to be an endless sequence of narrow hallways and stairs. Losh perched between Reyna's ears. His warm glow lit the way forward like a mining cap, revealing a passage that couldn't have been farther from the grand cathedral that lay above. The roofs were low enough that Sorrel had to move at a crouch. The walls were tight and close, and still rough with the tool marks of their creation. This wasn't a place to impress. This was a hastily dug means of entry and escape.

Losh clutched anxiously at Reyna's long red hair and muttered to himself. Even sounds of anxiety were oddly musical in his native language. The mountain trembled as Boviss continued to rage in his lair above.

"It is all right, Losh," Wren assured the little creature. "The dragon can't get us."

The fairy shook his head. "Not dragon. Cave. Cave bad. Tight. Close."

"It must be *enormous* to you," Reyna said.

"No. Sky big. World big. Cave small. Cave *cage*. Losh hate," Losh muttered unhappily.

"We'll find our way out just as soon as we can," Reyna said.

"I am not so sure that we will," Sorrel said, finally standing again as they entered a natural bit of cavern.

Her twins looked to her.

"Why not, Mama?" Reyna asked.

"We rescued you," Wren said.

Sorrel adjusted the chains she carried. Her eyes scanned across the cavern they'd found their way to. The ledge the three of them were on was leveled a bit, but otherwise a natural outcropping. Unlike the rest of their escape route thus far, the way forward was not clear. There were no steps, no rungs. All Sorrel could find to suggest how the dwarves had come or gone from this point was a pair of stout metal rings set into the stone.

"Can your fairy friend see if there is somewhere to climb down to?" Sorrel said.

"What do you say, Losh?" Reyna asked.

The fairy nodded and buzzed down into the darkness below. As he flitted about, Sorrel crossed her arms.

"When I tell you stories of Swift, the stories end. Swift does something clever. Swift learns a lesson. And then it is over until the next story," she said.

"Yes!" Wren said. "Maybe, now that you're safe, you can give us the big long story we earned by—"

"Wren. Listen. What do I tell you about the stories?" Sorrel asked.

"That stories are stories and life is life," the twins answered together.

"One of the ways that a story is not life is, in life, the story doesn't end. You freed me from Boviss. That is not the end. There will not be a safe place for you or me. And the other malthropes? There will not be a safe place for them either."

"What? No. Why?" Reyna said.

"Boviss is petty. Boviss is cruel. He will be angry that he lost me. He will make someone pay. If it can't be me, it will be someone else. It will be the Reds and the Fennecs. He will teach them a lesson. Not immediately, but in time."

Losh buzzed back up. "Losh protect desert children! Not let bad happen."

"Losh is right," Wren said. "We can't let bad things happen to the malthropes. We only *just* found our kind. We can't let them die. Not because of us!"

"Isn't there anything we can do?" Reyna asked.

Sorrel looked to the fairy. "Is there a way onward?"

He looked to her with as stern a look as his tiny and pixieish face could manage. "Down. Not far."

She huffed a breath and started to unwrap the chain from around her. "I will lower you down," Sorrel said.

"But is there anything we can do?" Wren asked.

"It is enough you saved me. More than most could do."

"But if we can save you, we can save them too, can't we? We've matched every challenge so far!" Reyna said.

The little malthrope reached out to take the chain her mother offered her. The moment her paw touched it, the chain glowed brightly and leaped. The shackle clicked open, struck like a snake, and snapped shut around Reyna's neck.

"Wh-what?" Reyna said, tugging at the chain as its links scaled down somewhat to become a more suitable size for her.

Sorrel took Reyna's paw and turned the palm up. Blood from her clever solution to the dwarf lock was still tacky on her fingers.

"Oh…" the little malthrope murmured.

"We'll leave it for now. Thinner chain will be easier to use. And maybe it will teach you that magic is more trouble than it is worth."

Sorrel wrapped the free end of the chain around one of the rings and started to lower the loop of chain down. Sure enough, she heard it clink down against the ledge Losh had spotted.

"Down. You first, Wren," Sorrel said.

Wren obeyed, sliding easily down the chain.

"But we can do something, can't we?" Reyna said, carefully easing herself onto the chain.

"Climb slow. You do not want to fall. That chain on your neck will kill you if you fall," Sorrel said.

Her second child made her way safely down. Sorrel followed, then set about swinging and looping the chain from the bottom to dislodge it from its anchor.

"Why aren't you answering, Mama?" Wren asked.

The way forward took on a shallow slope. Losh led the way, though he drifted backward, eyes fixed on Sorrel as though in pointing out Boviss would take revenge on the Fennecs, she was somehow the one who had told the dragon to do it.

"Did I save myself? Or did you save me?" she asked.

"We saved you," they replied.

"So maybe you tell me, then. What should we do?"

The twins looked to each other. After a moment, their expressions dropped a bit and they turned back to Sorrel.

"We hide in the tunnels," Reyna said.

"Find food and water here, and stay until we can find some way to keep clear of Boviss," Wren agreed.

Sorrel tipped her head. "That is what we should do. But is it what you want to do?"

"What we want doesn't matter," Reyna said. "What matters is what's safe."

Sorrel didn't quite remember teaching that lesson, but it was parroted back as though they'd heard it a thousand times.

"Maybe, this time, you tell your mother what you would do if you *could* do what you wanted."

The pair was silent for a few minutes, unsure of how to answer. When the answer finally came, Wren blurted it angrily.

"I want to stop playing the game!"

Sorrel gave him a surprised look. Even Reyna seemed surprised.

"Mama, we play the game every day. And every day we get a little better. It helps us learn to stay safe. It helps us learn to stay alive. But that's all it helps us learn!" he said.

"That is enough," Sorrel said.

"Maybe it is, but… maybe if we played a different game, we could do more than survive. Maybe we're playing the wrong game."

"Yes…" Reyna said, realization creeping in. "Mama, you played the game just right, and you still got captured."

"Because of the fairy. I didn't expect a fairy," she said. "Now we need to add that to the game."

"But that'll just teach us to do what we were already doing. Just run and hide. Always. Run and hide today so we can run and hide tomorrow. Games just keep the same things happening," Reyna said.

"The Fennecs and the Reds, they're playing a game that's keeping them scraping to survive and always fighting each other," Wren said.

"They're playing Boviss's game," Sorrel said with a nod.

"We're all just playing our own games. Nothing changes if you keep playing the same game," Wren said.

"We need a new game," Reyna said.

"What will the new game be?" Sorrel asked.

"I don't know," Reyna said. "But it'll be one we play with the Reds."

"And the Fennecs," Wren added.

"All of us together," Reyna nodded. "And, at least at first, we play it against Boviss."

Sorrel raised her eyebrows. "The Fennecs captured us. The Reds would not have us. Boviss would burn us to dust. You want a game that has us find a way to make friends of our enemies and fight a monster that has them both cowering in its shadow?"

"You asked what we would do if we could do what we want," Wren said.

"That's what we want." Reyna huffed. "We just can't do it."

Sorrel stepped ahead of them, turned, and crouched before them.

"It is a dangerous game. A game we've never played before. And a game we don't know how to win. It is dangerous. It is a bad idea."

They nodded and lowered their heads.

"We will play it," Sorrel said.

They looked up, a mixture of confusion and excitement on their faces.

"Really?" Reyna said.

"But it's not safe!" Wren said.

"There isn't any safe game anymore. If we want to be safe, we have to make a safe place. I do not like how the other malthropes acted, but they are malthropes. If *I* could have what I want, it would be to have you grow up surrounded by your kind. And besides, no one else will help us. And no one else will help them."

"So what will we do? How will we win?" Reyna asked.

She tousled their hair. "We have until we reach the villages to figure it out. Now let us go."

#

Boviss stalked through his lair. His eyes swept over the mounds of his hoard. Every nugget of missing gold, every weapon, every bit of armor that had been stolen burned at him. Jagged stone lay in piles beside his precious bed. Chunks of what had once been that hideous statue were buried among the gold and silver. He could feel that items heavy with enchantment had been shattered, broken, their mystic value squandered. This was an affront. It was disrespect that must not be allowed to stand. Flame roiled between his teeth as he approached the towering exit and cast his eyes out over the landscape.

"That insect. That scum…" he growled, fresh plumes of fire curling between his lips with each word. "I spared her life. I let her feast on my scraps. And this is how I am repaid!"

He'd baked and clawed at the wall through which the creatures had escaped for better than an hour, too blinded by his own rage to recall that it was the same blasted place that had kept the last wave of dwarves from crunching between his jaws. If he'd not been able to break through then, he wouldn't be able to now. And all the while his fury had built. Nothing. No living thing in his long life had done something like this before. None had dared. None would have lived past the first motion to do so. But she had. He drew in a breath. Two more scents mixed with her own. They were similar to her own and to each other, but unique all the same. Family.

His eyes narrowed as he set them upon the patch of landscape he knew to hold the Fennec village.

"They offered her to me… In place of food, they offered her."

He clenched his teeth tight. Flames shot in brilliant jets between them. Now his eyes shifted to the forest, where the Red malthropes hid.

"And she was of their kind. A child of the forest. I let them shelter in my shadow for so long. I allowed them to worship me and answered their most fervent prayer. I offered them *safety*. I offered them my protection. And this hideous act is their doing. They shall pay for this."

His gaze shifted to the middle distance. For the moment, his focus was on the thoughts and considerations swirling in his own mind. The fury did not fade. But something new layered atop it. A realization.

"But not before I find her…"

Boviss spread his wings and launched into the sky. He would hunt the blasted creature down. He would stalk the forests and mountains in search of their scent. In time, he would find them. And when they were nothing but dust and bones, those like them would suffer. Oh, how they would suffer.

#

A full day had passed. Sorrel, the twins, and Losh had yet to see the sun again. The mountain was not a maze. There was no getting lost in it. The tunnels both natural and manufactured did little branching and were clearly marked with dwarf writing. One need only take the wrong turn a few times to realize which markings meant dead end and which implied an exit. But these were passages made by, and for, dwarves. Dwarves cared little for the surface. They delved ever deeper. Deserted tunnels curled deeper into the ground. Here and there the malthropes found food left by the workers who had abandoned this place. But none of the paths led to the surface. Clearly the place that Boviss had claimed as his own was the one place that the dwarves had intended to face the surface world.

The Story of Sorrel

By now the group was weary. They were still heavily weighed down with their bits of stolen hoard. Sorrel once again wore the chain, a drop of blood having returned it to her neck. She coiled it about her body like a mountain climber's rope to avoid tripping over its free end.

Losh's dull glow wavered and wobbled as they marched down a fresh tunnel. He blinked bleary, red-rimmed eyes and gazed at a wall. His little fingers jutted toward the gray stone, and he released a warbling trill that ended in a petite hiccup.

"That's a wall, Losh," Reyna said.

He flitted over and landed on Reyna's head, hand still extended. "Out," he said, once again punctuating it with a hiccup.

"Maybe he needs more of this stuff," Wren said, sloshing a dark purple glass bottle.

Losh's eyes lit up, and he darted toward the bottle, hands extended. Sorrel stopped him with a raised hand and took the bottle from her son.

"He's had enough for now, I think," she said.

"But it's the only thing we found down here that he likes to eat!" Reyna said.

"If fairies need to drink brandy to live, I know why they seem so foolish," Sorrel said.

"No fool," Losh said, shaking his head and buzzing toward the wall again. "Out!"

This time he was far more specific. His little finger indicated a narrow crack in the wall. Sorrel leaned toward it and sniffed.

"There is… yes. There is fresh air."

She balled up some chain on her fist and knocked on the wall. The sound that echoed back was subtly different. There wasn't much wall there.

"Give the pick to me," Sorrel instructed. "We'll dig through this wall."

"I can do it, Mama!" Wren said. "I'm good with the pick."

He marched up to the wall and raised the tool. Before he could bring it down, the mountain trembled lightly around them. It had done so with great regularity during their journey. The relative softness of the trembling was the only real indication they had that they were getting farther away from the dragon as he raged.

"Won't he hear us?" Wren said. "Won't he *find* us?"

Sorrel thought for a moment. "Boviss cannot find us here. The place is too small. And here, smell. The air from outside? No strong smell of him. He does not know where to find us. And will we let him find us?"

"No," they replied in unison.

"No, we will not."

The tunnel trembled again. Sorrel placed a hand on a shoulder of each of her children.

"But if you are frightened, you wait until the mountain shakes. Dig then. If *he* smashes the mountain, he won't hear *us* smash the mountain."

Now that there was a plan, Wren nodded and held his pick ready for the next rumble.

"Mama?" Reyna said.

"Yes, little one."

"Losh little!" Losh blurted.

Sorrel glared at the drunken fairy, then looked back to her daughter. "What do you need to say?"

"I was afraid of… do you remember the story you told us? Swift and the fastest prey?"

She nodded. "Of course I remember it. And what is the lesson the story teaches you?"

"If you can go to the place you know the prey will be, it doesn't matter how fast the prey is, you will catch it," both twins quoted.

"That's right."

"So why does Boviss stay here? Why doesn't he go to the villages? I don't *want* him to. I don't want the people to get hurt. But you said he would take your escape out on them. And he must know we will head there."

The mountain shook again. Wren pounced on the opportunity to drive the head of the pick into the stone. The mystic tool devoured the wall. He managed only three swings, but they each punched a fist-size hole in the stone. The last of them punched fully through to a tunnel on the other side that brought with it a puff of undeniably fresh air.

"Out!" Losh crowed. He flitted up and out of the hole, leaving the malthropes in darkness save for the jagged glow through his tiny escape route. He poked his head back in. "Follow!" he insisted.

The Story of Sorrel

"Drunk fairies aren't very bright," Reyna observed.

"*Losh bright!*" the fairy countered.

To illustrate his point he flared his glow until it stung their eyes. Sorrel irritably snatched him from the hole and stuffed him into one of Reyna's pockets, where he jingled against the stolen gold stowed there.

"Stay there until the hole is big enough for all of us," Sorrel instructed.

The fairy buzzed his wings in a bid for freedom, but his booze-addled brain gently suggested maybe napping in a cozy pocket wasn't the worst thing in the world at the moment. He cuddled low and dulled his glow to a soft glimmer.

With the interruption over, she looked to Reyna. "You want to know why Boviss doesn't attack the city now?" Sorrel said.

"Yes. We may have tricked him, but someone doesn't live as long and grow as big as him without being wise."

"When one grows as big and as strong and as old as him, sometimes one gets *too* wise. Sometimes someone knows too much about how good they are. They start to *need* to be big and strong, and *need* to be wise. And for Boviss, there is something more. He needs to know that *others* know he is big and strong and wise."

"What do you mean?"

"You were with the Fennecs, yes?"

"Yes."

"And they talk about Boviss the way they talk about a god. They fear him. They praise him. All that."

"Yes."

"I was with Boviss. He *needs* fear and praise."

"So he'll never destroy the village?"

"I did not say that," Sorrel said.

Another tremble sent Wren's pick into the wall. When he was through, the hole was just large enough for the twins, but it would take another few swings to widen it for Sorrel.

"Then what do you mean?" Reyna asked.

"He will do bad things to the village. Maybe he will kill most. Maybe he will kill all of them and find a new village. But he won't do it while we breathe. We are the ones who escaped him. We are proof he is not perfect."

"But he knows we'll go to the village. He can go there and wait for us. He can tell them to turn us over."

"No. Because then the village will know we escaped. He will not let the village know he is weak at all."

"But that means… he's going to scour the mountain, the forest, the desert. He'll follow us no matter where we go."

"Yes."

Both Wren and Reyna tried to put on a brave face, but the fear was bone deep and it showed. Sorrel crouched and hugged them close.

"You remember the stories, yes?"

"Yes," they answered.

"And you remember the game. How you lost when you lost. How you won when you won, yes?"

"Yes."

"And we got away from Boviss once, yes?"

"Yes."

"So he is smart, but we are smarter. He is faster. He is stronger. But we are sneakier. We are sly. No one can run away like we can. No one can hide like we do. No one can smell the wind and watch the shadows like we can. Boviss can follow all he likes. He will not find us. And when we get to the other malthropes? Well… I don't know what we will do. But we will find a way to make them as smart as we are. We will find a way to make them see what Boviss really is. And then? An army of malthropes as clever as you and me?" She shook her head. "Nothing, not even a dragon is as mighty as that. So we get our people. All of them. We show them. And together, we hunt the dragon."

#

A lifetime. So often, one thinks of a lifetime as a very, very long time. Ideally, it is, but it need not be. Reyna and Wren each had a lifetime of training in the art of predators and prey. Sorrel had years more training than they did, but still just a lifetime. And now, those three lifetimes of knowledge, practice, and experience were being put to the test. If they'd learned their past lessons well, there was just a chance that for each of them, a lifetime would be a very long time indeed. But at the moment, the lifetime was beginning to feel terribly short.

The hole Wren had widened for them led to an air shaft. A tricky climb brought them to the surface, much to the relief of their fairy friend. From there, things became far more harrowing. The shaft led to a stretch of mountain at the very fringe of the forest. It offered barely a hint of cover from the beast who sought them. High above them, their former captor and new hunter stalked over the face of the mountain. He was distant, but his sheer enormity made him quite visible. The sight of him crawling along the sheer cliffs of the mountain, sniffing and licking at the stone in search of his prey, awakened ancient fears deep in their minds. And there was something far worse. Just as the malthropes had had a lifetime of learning to hunt and hide, so too did Boviss have a lifetime of predatory experience. And for him, that lifetime was longer than lesser creatures could imagine. That time brought more than expertise, more than skill. It brought a kind of second sight, an instinct that defied understanding. As their eyes fell upon him, even half a mountain away, he seemed to feel their gaze. His eyes shifted toward them. His wings spread.

The longest days in the lives of the malthropes began with that moment. Losh stayed with them, teasing the wind into shapes that concealed their scent. Each step was careful and measured. Not a hint of a footprint was left to be found or followed. For the first time, Wren and Reyna were playing the game *with* their mother. Not just a simple demonstration, but a very real, life-or-death game of hiding and retreating. They learned more in those days of pursuit than in the previous year. And it was barely enough. Whenever they thought they'd lost Boviss, a cold shadow would sweep over them. Seldom did an hour pass that they didn't smell his scent on the breeze. At times, he was near enough for his breath to rustle the leaves of the trees around them.

Then the moment came. As though the fleeing malthropes had stepped past some invisible line etched into the forest floor, the dragon wheeled back toward his mountain.

"Where is he going?" Wren whispered, eyes wide and fingers tight about the handle of his stolen pick.

"Is he hungry, maybe? Or tired?" Reyna offered.

Sorrel watched the dragon go. Her mind churned. "This other village. The village of Reds. It is near, isn't it?" Sorrel said.

The twins gazed at the forest. They sampled the air for something other than the dragon's scent for the first time in ages.

"It is still far. But we are heading in the right direction. Another day at the speed we've been going and we will reach it," Reyna said.

"And how far if we were able to run?" Sorrel asked.

"A few hours? Maybe less," Wren judged.

"Close enough that villagers might encounter him," Sorrel said. "They will have seen him already. But much farther and they might encounter him. I think he wants to avoid that. Too many questions. Too close to admitting weakness."

"But he's followed us this far," Reyna said. "He knows that we're bound to reach the village now."

Sorrel nodded. "Now is the dangerous time."

"*Now* is the dangerous time?" Wren said, visibly trembling. "But the last few days—"

"The last few days we were being hunted by a hunter after his prey. Nothing new about that. He would do what a hunter would do. But now he knows there is nothing he can do. If he hunts farther, the malthropes will wonder why he has come to them. If he doesn't, we will reach his people and they learn the truth. We cannot know what he will do now. Maybe nothing? Maybe he will burn the forest to the ground."

"S-so what do we do?" Reyna asked.

Sorrel shook her head. "Nothing changes. We go to the village. We do as we planned. But we keep our eyes open. We perk our ears. … And I head south."

"But the village of the Reds is so close!" Reyna said.

She turned to her daughter. "I know. And that's why I must go south. You go to the forest village."

"But you should come with us!"

"Why? Because it is close? Will we be safe there?"

The twins shook their heads.

"We won't be safe anywhere. Not from Boviss," Wren said.

"Boviss turned away. For now, Boviss thinks we will go to the village of the Reds. He thinks we will *all* go there. And when is it good to go where our hunters think we are going?"

"Never," they answered in unison.

"So I will go south," Sorrel said. "It will give him another trail. It will give us another chance."

"Across the open desert?" Wren asked.

"Do you even know the way?" Reyna asked.

"I spent time there. I was taken there. I can find the way. And now is the best time, while Boviss thinks he knows where we are and has turned his eyes away." She turned to the flitting fairy. "Will you help me?"

Losh crossed his arms and considered the question. "Losh like Reyna and Wren. Reyna and Wren like Mama."

"Sorrel," she said.

"Reyna and Wren say Mama." Losh nodded once. "Losh help Mama."

"But… but we just saved you…" Wren said to Sorrel.

"We don't want to split up again. Not so soon," Reyna said.

"A dragon took me away and I survived. This? This is nothing."

"But what do we do?" Wren asked.

"You go to the forest village. You persuade them to meet somewhere both sides know. The place of the offering. I will do the same."

"But how will we do that?" Wren asked.

"You are clever. You do not need me to do your thinking. But get them there. One week from today. I will do the same."

"But—" Reyna objected.

"No but. You came from there to here. You came from here to Boviss. You escaped the Fennecs, you escaped the Reds, and you helped me to escape the dragon. You can do this."

"But the Fennecs will—" Wren said.

"The Fennecs will shake hands with the Reds. We will make sure."

"But what if you fail? And what if we fail?" Reyna asked.

"Then we all die. And they die too, probably. So we will not fail." She pulled them close and gave each a loving lick on their head. "You are ready," she said. "And you are my clever little ones. You can do this. Now go."

The twins looked up to her. They paused only long enough to give her a tight hug. And then, with a few bounding leaps, they were gone. Silent, invisible. Sorrel's lips curled into a grin.

"Make your mother proud." She looked up to Losh. "You know the way back to the Fennecs, yes?"

"Yes. But Losh not lead—"

"You have rules. I don't care. If we do this right, Boviss will not hurt any malthrope ever again. If we do not, he will do terrible things to all malthropes."

Losh scratched his head. "I lead then."

Sorrel nodded and dashed to the south. Losh huffed.

"Things get hard for Losh fast…"

Chapter 13

Without the dragon breathing down their necks, and with little reason to move stealthily, Reyna and Wren covered the remaining distance to the forest village in no time at all. When they'd left this place, they'd been pursued by the Reds. Along the way, they'd expected to encounter them again. No malthrope worth its salt would have given up on the search so quickly. But there'd been no one. Not until they came upon the subtle signs of the village itself did they even catch the scent of their own kind.

Wren eyed the simple roads and gardens. All were seemingly abandoned.

"Where is everyone?" Wren asked.

"Would you be out and about if a dragon was flying around all the time?" Reyna asked.

He glared at her. "That just answers why they aren't here, not where they *went*."

"So we follow our noses." Reyna sniffed. "There are so many, and they must be near."

They crept, noses low to the ground, through what appeared to be an entirely empty town. The scent was certainly strong, and getting stronger. The paths were fresh, and numerous. They showed uncharacteristic carelessness, leading quite directly toward a single point with little regard for how easily they would be followed.

The many trails converged on a single tree. It was enormous, older by far than any of the others in the village and the surrounding forest. The towering, ancient tree stood atop a large hill at the center of the village. As they drew near, they discovered that heavy stone doors had been set into the slope of the hill. The doors were surrounded by scattered soil, as though they'd been hastily opened and shut quite recently.

Wren's ears twitched as he stared down at the door. "Do you hear them?" he asked quietly.

"They're there. They're underground." Reyna searched the door for some means to open it, but there was nothing obvious. "We really *are* good at hiding."

"We don't have time for hiding," Wren said. He kicked at the door and demanded, "Hello! Let us in! We have to talk!"

Startled chatters echoed from behind the door. A moment later, some scratching suggested the people within were shifting about. Then there came a familiar voice.

"Wren? Reyna?" called Hask.

"Yes! Come out, we need to talk."

"No! Boviss is out! He is prowling. He hasn't done it for years. It is an ill omen. You brought this upon us."

"That's what we're here about!" Reyna said. "We need to find a way to deal with him."

"Boviss is power! Boviss is might given form! He cannot be dealt with. We can only hope that we can find a way to quell his rage."

Wren growled. "If you won't come out, we are coming in."

"You cannot! This is our mightiest stronghold. If anything can protect us from Boviss's rage, for even a day, it is this place. You will never—"

Wren didn't wait for him to finish. With a practiced motion, he hefted the pick from his shoulder. A single swing of the enchanted piece of dwarven workmanship punched neatly through the door. Voices shouted in fear and skittered away. A second blow shattered the door entirely. Its remnants crumbled into the hole.

He shouldered the pick and made ready to drop down. Reyna motioned for him to step back. It was a wise precaution. Had he not retreated, the arrow that hissed out of the hole would have been buried in his chest.

Hask emerged from the doorway, bow in hand. He spotted Wren first and took aim. Reyna acted quickly, swiping with her stolen sword. The single, inexpert slice with the unique weapon was enough to cut neatly through the bow.

Before the adult malthrope could recover from the shock of what had occurred, the twins pounced. They each grasped an arm and hauled him out of the doorway. Wren wrestled him to the ground and put the tip of the pick to his throat. Reyna stood over him, sword held at the ready.

"H-how?" Hask asked.

"We've been through a lot, Hask," Wren said.

"We've been to Boviss's lair and back," Reyna said.

"Impossible!" he said.

Reyna turned to the doorway. The scampering of feet suggested reinforcements would be arriving soon. They were going to have to get a good deal more persuasive, and fast, because holding one of their villagers hostage wasn't going to help with negotiations. A thought occurred to her.

"This village needs gold, right?" she said. "You have all the food you need for Boviss, but you haven't got a nugget of gold to give."

"The Fennecs have it all. We can't get any," Hask said.

Reyna dug her paw into one of the many pockets in her layers of clothing. She threw down a handful of glittering gold and jewels stolen from Boviss's hoard. The look in Hask's eyes was that of someone who had finally found an oasis after weeks in the desert.

"And there's more where that came from," Wren said, tossing a handful of his own gold. "But only if you listen."

Armed malthropes poured from the stronghold beneath the tree's door, weapons drawn. Reyna held her weapon in one paw, her inexperience more than evident. In the other, she held a fistful of stolen precious gems. Wren kept the pick to Hask's throat, but similarly fished out a nugget of gold the size of a goose egg.

For a few tense moments, no one moved. No one spoke. Reyna broke the stalemate.

"We can tell you where we got this gold, and these weapons. And we can tell you where to get enough for *all* of you. But only if you listen, and you don't kill us."

Another few moments passed before anyone moved again. This time it was Hask. He nodded to the others. They backed away and lowered their weapons.

Wren and Reyna each took a breath.

"Now there is a lot to say," Wren said, easing up on the pick.

"And you have to listen to *all* of it," Reyna said.

"We can prove it all."

"But none of it will matter if you don't listen to what we have to say about what comes next."

All in attendance nodded. Wren and Reyna nodded to each other as well. They each offered a paw to Hask and pulled him from the ground.

"Now listen close," Wren said.

"We don't have time to do this twice."

#

Days later, a windstorm scoured the desert. It did not, however, scour Sorrel. When the wind reached her, it obligingly stopped and the wind-swept sand sprinkled harmlessly to the ground. The harsh wind and obscuring debris made for exceptional cover, however. As such, Sorrel was able to run without concern for the trail she'd leave behind. That was good, because with the weight of the stolen goods and the chain she still wore, it would have been a very long trip otherwise.

"I am beginning to understand just how helpful you fairies are," Sorrel remarked.

"Mama owe Losh," he replied.

"I suppose I do," she said, reluctantly.

Sorrel stopped to catch her breath and survey her surroundings. The stretch of desert was beginning to look and smell quite familiar. On top of all the other valuable tricks he knew, Losh was a fine guide.

She tugged at the chains and the shackle that held it to her neck. Though it meant hauling the heaps of enchanted metal much, much farther than either of the twins would have, she couldn't bring herself to inflict the chain upon them. It had crossed her mind to try applying it to Losh to see if it would be reducible to a more manageable size, but the little creature already treated her in a rather surly manner. She didn't want to risk him changing his mind about lending a hand.

Her ears flicked. Somewhere beneath the wailing wind, she could hear the patter of cunning paws. She was slowly and steadily being surrounded. Any other time, she wouldn't have allowed such a thing to happen. But her long journey had given her ample time to mull over what she wanted to do when she arrived, and how they were likely to treat her when they encountered her. If she was correct, it wouldn't matter if they surrounded her. If she was incorrect, she would be captured, and one way or another, killed.

She would thus take pains to ensure she was correct.

Shadowy forms began to emerge from the storm, weapons held at the ready. Sorrel held her ground. Six of the Fennecs surrounded her. When they were satisfied she wasn't going to attack, a seventh figure emerged. It was the chieftain.

He looked up to her, eyes squinted against the lingering wind at the edge of Losh's influence.

"Do you remember me?" Sorrel asked, a dash of challenge in her voice.

"I do."

"And do you remember what you *did* to me?"

"I do. How is it that you returned?" the chieftain asked. "You were an offering. A sacrifice."

"I escaped."

"Impossible. Boviss is all powerful."

She crossed her arms. "I knew you wouldn't believe my word, but surely you will believe your own senses. Am I not the same creature you captured? Am I not flesh and blood, standing before you?"

"You are."

"Then either Boviss really is as powerful as you believe, and he chose to let me free; or he is as mortal and fallible as you and I, and I was able to escape him. That means you are risking his ire by threatening someone who travels with his blessing, or you are threatening the one creature in this world who can teach you how to defeat him. I do not think you can afford to threaten me any further in either case."

"We have seen Boviss soaring, searching. You will bring ruin upon us by coming here."

"Ruin is already upon you. I heard the demands of the dragon when you handed me over. You could not spare food enough for him before. And now he requires twice as much. Even if I'd not escaped, come the next full moon you would be offering more of your village to feed his hunger, or else watching your people starve as your food goes to him. But I have a plan to rid you of him forever."

"Rid us of him… He is our protector!"

"A protector does not harvest those he protects. He is a tyrant. And the time has come for an uprising. If we defeat him, what right did he have to claim to be your protector? And if we fail? He would have killed us anyway."

"You would have us follow you? You who wears chains?"

"You sent me in a cage. I returned in chains. Neither could keep me from my freedom." She leaned down to him. "Imagine what I could have done if I'd not been imprisoned. Imagine what *we* could do if we worked together."

"We would never reach him."

"I know the way to his lair. And I know a secret way inside."

"And how—"

"I don't think well with spears pointed at me. And I've dashed across the desert to reach you. Ask me inside. Offer me a drink." She glanced aside. "And something for the fairy here. Maybe you'll like what you hear."

The Fennecs considered her words.

"My twins are up north, making the same offer to the Red malthropes as I am to you." Sorrel dug a hand into a pocket and revealed a fistful of gems. "They have a heap of these. I know you don't need them, but the Reds do. And if you don't listen to me, and the Reds listen to them, then what do you think will happen to you?"

After a tense silence, the Chieftain chattered to the others and they stepped aside.

"You say what you want to say. But if we do not like it—"

"You won't like it," Sorrel said. "It won't be easy. But you'll do it. Because you are malthropes. And malthropes aren't fools. They know how to dig their way out of a bad situation. You just have to be willing to work. Now, let us talk."

#

Reyna and Wren sat upon the great stone slab where not so long ago their mother had been offered. The random assemblage of stolen clothes, valuables, weapons, and armor were gone. Now they were dressed very much as the other Reds were. Leather armor joined the scattered pieces of stolen dwarf equipment, and deep green capes were layered over the top. Wren still carried his pick, and Reyna her sword, but the rest of their outfits made them look very much like a part of the entourage of six that had accompanied them. One was the village chieftain. The rest were her heavily armed guards. Three water fairies had also accompanied them, the better to hide their trails.

"How much longer do you expect us to wait?" the Red chieftain asked.

"Until they get here," Wren said.

"It won't be long. Today is the day Mama said we should meet, so today is the day she will be here," Reyna said.

"It isn't even night yet," Wren said. "Give them time."

"He will not come," the chieftain said. "The Fennecs are proud and strong-willed. They will not come here knowing they cannot succeed without our help."

"You came here knowing you'd need *their* help," Reyna countered.

"Mama survived in Boviss's lair, and she escaped with *our* help," Wren said. "She can persuade some malthropes to do the right thing. She can do *anything*."

"We have been rivals with the Fennecs for ages," the chieftain said. "What makes you believe you and your mother can get us to set that rivalry aside?"

"Because you've been playing the wrong game," Reyna said. "And all you need to see is that there's a better game to play."

Wren hopped up. "There! See?"

The others turned. It was subtle, but a patch of the dry ground in the distance flickered with motion. Before long, four figures could be seen hurrying toward them. One was clearly Sorrel, standing a head and shoulders above the Fennecs. Another was the Fennec chieftain, and the remainder were guards. A familiar fairy joined them. As they approached, the armed members of both the forest and desert envoys became tense. Hands went to the grips of weapons. Postures stiffened. Teeth clenched.

"Calm down!" Wren snapped.

"We're here to talk, not fight," Reyna said.

The twins hopped down and dashed to their mother. She crouched and pulled them into a hug.

"We did it, Mama! We convinced them," Reyna said.

"We had to give them the gold and stuff. I hope that's okay," Wren said.

"Whatever it takes, my little ones." Sorrel raised her head and looked to the Red malthropes. "My children told you what we had to do?"

"They did," the Red chieftain said. "It is madness."

"Madness? Madness is fighting with your own kind to feed a dragon who doesn't need the meal. Madness is paying a dragon who doesn't need the gold. What I am offering you is freedom." She jingled the chain she still wore wrapped around her body. "This? Your dragon put this on me not so long ago. I am already tired of it. You have been wearing your chains for far longer."

"You would have us kill our savior," the forest Chieftain said.

"What has he saved you from? Hmm? From the elves? Do you see any elves here? From the humans? The dwarves? Who is fighting you? Hmm? I saw other cages in the lair. How many of you have died because of him, and how many have been saved because of him? Starved because you needed the food to feed him? Killed by one another because you tried to steal what you needed? No more."

"Sorrel has spoken at length. Her plan will not be simple, but it has a chance," the desert Elder said. "And having escaped him, she *will* have angered him. We will face Boviss's ire whether we try the plan or not. And even if we do not, I do not suppose *you* have the gold to meet his requirements, and I know *we* do not have the flesh. We will lose people come the full moon regardless. The people of Burrow choose battle. What of you?"

The forest Elder shifted her weight. "If we had time to see if this was true…"

"There is not time," Sorrel said. "We do this, all of us, at once, or it is not done."

The desert Elder stepped forward.

"We have fought one another for too long." He held out a hand. "The time has come to fight together."

His counterpart considered the offered hand for a moment, then reached out. "So be it."

Sorrel clapped. "Good! Then we start as soon as we can. We leave immediately. I will show you all where to go, where to hide. It will take every one of us, and all the time we have. Here is what we will need…"

Chapter 14

Boviss sat in the mouth of his lair, eyes on the mountains, waiting. Weeks had passed since he had lost Sorrel. He had been simmering with fury. She was with them. Most likely with the forest children. Creatures of a kind tended to seek one another out. They would have questions. Perhaps they would even have doubts. His lips curled a bit, revealing more of his terrible teeth. He would teach them not to question him, and never again to doubt him. As the moon revealed itself, he spread his wings.

"They shall learn the price of disobedience."

He thrust himself from his perch. What had taken days for the fleeing malthrope to cover would take him little more than hours. He flew lazily, luxuriously. The price for this offering was double what it had been. Neither would be able to cover it. Even without the terrible plans he had in store for them to punish them for Sorrel's actions, they would be trembling at the thought of his arrival. Better to let them suffer, let them see his shadow sweep the land. Let them boil in the anticipation.

A leisurely flight eventually took him to the place of offering. His eyes set upon the twin slabs of stone below. They were empty.

"What?" Boviss roared.

He tucked his wings and plummeted. When he struck the ground, it was with force enough to shatter one of the slabs and heave the other from its mounting. Nothing. Not a scrap of food. Not a nugget of gold. And no malthrope from either the forest or the desert.

"How dare they… *How dare they?!*"

He leaped into the sky and headed north. As he flew, his mind roiled with anger. Worse, it simmered with uncertainty. What had happened? How could *no one* have arrived with an offering. Perhaps some disaster might have kept the forest children from attending, or perhaps the same for the desert children. But both? That both had abandoned their obligation stank of agreement. *Agreement.* After all these years of carefully playing them against each other, that they might have agreed to spit in the face of their benefactor was more than he could bear. If these ungrateful, pitiful, meaningless creatures believed they could work against him, he would show them what awaited those who trifled with him.

Perhaps they were foolish enough to believe that he didn't know where to find them if he wished to. The forest was enormous, and the piddling little nothings were quite good at hiding. Particularly with their precious fairies to stir the wind and foul their scent. But even the constant influence of the little things wouldn't be enough to hide the scent of a whole village. And even if they could, he already knew where to find them. He'd always known.

Mighty, majestic trees rose up beneath him. He watched them whisk by until he saw the one he was waiting for. Enormous, ancient. Of course they would have built their village around it. Perhaps the small-minded things even *worshiped* it, the deity he had come to replace. In a moment, it would no longer matter.

Boviss opened his maw and belched forth a stout column of flame. The yellow-and-orange tongue of destruction washed through the trees like a wave. In the blink of an eye, the place that the malthropes had called home was entirely consumed in flame. He circled around and blasted another swath, carving a second line of flame across the heart of their village. A few more bursts of flame would be all it would take to completely eliminate the village and all its inhabitants. But that was not his aim. If he killed them all, there would be no one left to suffer, no one left to come to him seeking forgiveness. His toys would be lost. Better to give them this horrid scar to remind them, in the years it would take to rebuild, just how potent his wrath could be.

It was a shame that the foliage was too dense for him to see their panic, their horror. But that was of little concern. He knew what was happening to them. That was enough. He could drink in the anguish of the desert creatures. He turned to the south and began the trek to the stretch of the desert they thought would keep them safe. After just a few hours more, he saw the rolling dunes and smelled the faint lingering scent of the Fennecs. They lacked a clear landmark like the tree for him to navigate by, and they were if anything even more skilled at concealing their home, but Boviss was a hunter above all else. He found his way first to where he believed the village to be, then put his senses to work finding precisely where they made their homes.

A short search was all it took for him to come upon the carefully concealed mounds and burrows where the desert creatures lived. He could almost respect them. Buried in the ground as they were, most creatures couldn't hope to threaten them. But he was no common beast. He drew in a breath and puffed his chest. Flames rolled from this nostrils and burst between his teeth. He blasted the ground and broiled the sand until it bubbled. His flames scoured half the village. Dunes started to slump down upon themselves as the burrows beneath collapsed. Any moment, like vermin, the other half of the village would scurry out of cover.

But that moment did not come. Even when the scrub grass had been seared away and much of the village lay as a crackled bowl of glass, not a single malthrope climbed from the rubble to beg for mercy. He dug his claws into the earth and tore open the tops of a few of the surviving burrows.

"Empty…" he seethed.

They had fled. Abandoned their homes. It was a wise precaution. Were he in their place, cowering in the shadow of a mighty creature they could not hope to satisfy, he would have sought some sort of refuge. But the entire village? Where had they gone?

His mind started to churn. What if the forest children had done the same? What if the village he had razed was empty? Things were happening that he had not anticipated. He did not like it. It had been centuries since he'd last felt as though something was beyond his control. Then that blasted newcomer escaped and…

The newcomer…

Boviss's claws cleaved the earth beneath him. This was her doing.

He launched himself skyward and turned his eyes to his mountain.

#

In half the time it had taken him to travel to the place of offering and exact his vengeance, Boviss returned to his lair. But he had wasted too much time reaching and attacking the malthropes who had not been there. Now dawn was beginning to color the sky. He swept his wings back and charged through the mouth of his home at a sprint, dashing through the cave tunnel to his inner sanctum. The air was heavy with their scent. They had been here. The malthropes had desecrated his home. And when he charged into the place that should hold his hoard…

"Empty?!" he bellowed.

He swept his head about, scanning the vault. There was nothing. Not a gem. Not a trinket.

"How!" he demanded, as though the walls themselves owed him the answer. "I was gone for mere hours! How could it all be gone?"

"Perhaps it is true what they say," echoed a confounding voice from deeper in his lair. "Malthropes are born thieves."

Boviss turned. The echo made it difficult to pinpoint where the sound was coming from, and the hundreds of different malthrope scents made it difficult to single out which belonged to the blasted newcomer.

"What do you think you have gained?" he growled. "Do you think I shall give up? It took me centuries to gather that wealth, but centuries are nothing to me. I shall have it back in due time. But not before I've ground each of your blasted kin to *dust* beneath my claws."

"You had them beneath your claws for long enough," Sorrel taunted.

Boviss followed the sound down another emptied corridor of his lair.

"It's your own fault, you know," Sorrel said. "You gave them what it took to do this."

"Oh?" Boviss rumbled. "Pray tell."

"We were already sneaky, but you forced us to be sneakier. You forced us to work with the fairies, to hide our scent. You starved us, taught us to live on the tiniest of scraps. You terrified us, taught us to live for days at a time without venturing from our burrows to see the light of day. You made us into precisely the sort of creatures who could lay in wait in the tunnels beneath your lair. For days. Waiting."

"The tunnels… So you have moved my wealth to the tunnels left by the dwarves."

"Where you will never be able to reach it. Always just beyond your reach."

He turned. The voice was closer now, but the halls were narrower. He seldom came to this distant corner of his lair. The dwarves had not mined it out to the same degree. It did not suit one of his size, but he continued.

"No. When I have roasted and devoured all but a handful of your kind, those who remain will beg for the opportunity to retrieve my hoard. And if I am generous, I will allow it. But you and your wretched brood will not live to see that day."

"Because that day will never come. But enough hiding."

A flash of light drew his attention. At the end of the tunnel to his right, a soft glimmer revealed itself. His eyes focused upon the form he'd been searching for, illuminated by the enchanted glow of chains still wrapped about her. His body acted of its own accord, breaking into a sprint. Fire poured from his mouth as he bounded toward her. His wings and legs scraped and smashed at the walls and columns, but he did not slow. Just when he was growing near enough for a lance of flame to reach her, she dropped from view, slipping down through one of the drains in the floor. Boviss slid to a stop. The bars that covered similar drains elsewhere in his lair had been sliced through, revealing a tight, dark tunnel. The glimmer of her torch was still visible within, shining against the trickle of water on the floor.

"Coward!" he bellowed, clawing at the floor. "You can't hide from me for long!"

"I won't have to," she called back.

He ceased his clawing for a moment, then slowly raised his head. The roof here was taller than the tunnel that led to it, vaulted a bit. And though none of the mystic lanterns was lit, the darkness above still sparkled. He opened his maw to blast a burst of flame, but it was too late. Dozens of malthropes, armed with the enchanted weapons that had until hours ago been precious pieces of his hoard, rained down upon him. Fennecs, Reds, and even the blasted children of the horrid newcomer dropped upon him. Weapons of supernatural strength and sharpness hacked and bit at him. The creatures swarmed him like insects. He shook and heaved, throwing them aside, but they bounded back. Blasts of fire sent them scattering, but there were simply too many. He couldn't clear them all away.

With each attack and retreat, more of the blasted things focused on his right foreleg. They hacked and chiseled, each attack managing the tiniest gouge in his tough hide. Finally, he felt something that reached past annoyance to genuine pain.

#

Amid the chaos of the attack, Wren hauled at the enchanted pick that he'd come to rely upon. His latest diving blow had driven it deep between the monster's scales. It had sunk into the white scar

Sorrel had instructed them to attack. When the sharp tip slid free, it sizzled with dark blood.

"Blood!" he cried. "We drew blood! Go, go!"

All at once, the assault ended. The malthropes flooded from the chamber down an adjoining tunnel. Behind them, Boviss rolled to his feet and released a roar that shook stones from the roof. Wren leaped around a turn just in time to escape a rush of flame.

"Here!" he called. "Take it!"

He tried to offer the pick to one of the full grown Reds who dashed ahead. Their long strides were making short work of the tunnel, but a lifetime in fear of a dragon's wrath had a way of robbing resolve from even the stoutest mind. The terrified malthropes, sapped of their will to fight by the raging creature, left Wren behind. Boviss slammed into the wall behind them. The passage shook. Even in a tunnel barely as large as himself, Boviss was nearly as fast as the malthropes. And even if he couldn't catch them, his flame eventually would.

"Wren! This way!"

He looked up to see his sister nestled in a groove that ran the length of the tunnel roof. There was no sense wondering how she had spotted it and found her way to it so quickly. She was Reyna; hiding was what she did best. He bounded from floor to wall, and from wall to carving, and finally scrambled across the roof. He snatched her outstretched paw just in time for her to pull him out of the tunnel ahead of a blast of flame.

"Quick, quick. We can still do it!" she hissed to him, leading the way down the groove.

Boviss thundered along below, but the other malthropes had made it clear. After a few more strides, the beast stopped and sniffed the air.

"Her brood…" Boviss said.

The twins stopped their scramble and held perfectly still. Boviss's massive head swept to and fro, then slowly tipped toward them. With a shaking paw, Reyna pulled her stolen sword from her belt and dragged it lightly across the tip of Wren's pick.

"We go. We split up. He can't catch both of us," Reyna said.

Wren nodded, then looked down to the hunter below. When the moment was right, he dropped.

It was a tight tunnel, and Boviss filled it almost completely. One could be excused for believing that there would be no way to escape the monster, no way to run or hide. But these were the children of Sorrel. They were trained from birth to make perfect use of every nook and cranny, to wait for the perfect time to move. The pair of them bounced and dashed from shadow to corner. Slashing claws came close enough to slice cloaks and rustle fur, but they continued without missing a step.

Ahead, Sorrel stood in the center of the next chamber. She straddled another of the gaps in the floor. Her eyes were wide and pleading.

"Now! Give it now!" she shouted.

Reyna dove from a shadow and heaved her short sword toward her mother. It skittered and slid. Sorrel lunged for it and snatched it up. Reyna hopped into the shadow of another column. Boviss continued past her. Now that he'd seen Sorrel, nothing else mattered. The twins watched from the shadows as the hulking monster stalked toward her. Fire curled from his nostrils as he approached the chamber that contained her. She held the short sword ready, eyes raised to meet the beast.

He paused before entering the chamber, sniffing the air but not daring to take his eyes from the insidious creature before him lest he lose her again.

"You are alone in the chamber. Not another trap. Your brothers and sisters have abandoned you," Boviss uttered.

"And you are fearful of entering a part of your own lair," Sorrel taunted. "You are afraid of us. True wisdom at last."

"Fearful… no. Aware. And that is more than you are worth," he said, stepping closer. "You have given me nothing to fear."

"Nothing?" she raised the sword. "We drew blood."

He stepped forward until his great head towered over her in the taller chamber.

"A single drop of blood. Two villages burnt to cinders. All of your kind doomed. And for a single drop of blood."

Sorrel smiled. "Sometimes a single drop is enough."

She made her move. Rather than swiping at him, she dragged the blade across the chain hanging from her neck. The links were no longer wrapped about her. They led down into the drain. Boviss's eyes widened. The chain took on a brilliant glow, surging up to the shackle around her neck and down into the floor. He reared back, but it was too late. The shackle snapped open and launched toward his neck. A dwarven enchantment forged untold years ago finally served the purpose for which it was crafted. The shackle grew large enough to fit Boviss's neck and snapped tight about his throat. One by one, the links of the chain grew to a size suitable to bind such a beast.

Sorrel, finally free of the chain again, sprang back, and not a moment too soon. The enraged dragon lunged at her. The growing links reached the gap in the floor and continued, lodging ever tighter into the stone of the mountain. Boviss's seemingly endless might finally met its match. The chain ground to a stop, hopelessly lodged in the earth. Anger robbed the dragon of logic and wisdom. He could have belched a flame to char Sorrel to ash where she stood, but all he could think of was getting free. He thrashed and tugged at the chain. Great claws slashed stone. A sweeping tail pounded the walls. Chunks of stone clattered down. Then, a single, pristine clang rang out. Boviss froze and looked to the source of the sound. A large ax, enchanted and of dwarven make, had driven itself into the stone of the floor. The dragon peered upward to the shuddering ceiling. It was positively *studded* with similar weapons. Easily half of the weapons in his hoard had been lashed, lodged, and mounted there. His thrashing had begun to bring the ceiling down. And the blades were coming with it.

His eyes turned to Sorrel. She grinned and swiped her claw across her throat.

"Dead."

Boviss's wits returned a moment too late to end her. She bounded aside as his flame lanced toward her. She dodged between clattering stones and into the hallway that held her children.

"Come, come! Fast!" she called.

Wren and Reyna joined their mother as they dashed for safety.

"Will it be enough, Mama?" Wren asked breathlessly, desperate to keep pace.

"It took all that we had and we barely broke his skin," Reyna said.

"We are fast and we are clever, we are not as strong as a dragon. A malthrope may not be able to swing an ax hard enough to kill him. But a mountain just may."

Far behind them, slabs of stone and hundreds of enchanted weapons rained down as the mountain claimed the creature who was once its king.

#

The Story of Sorrel

Malthropes rushed from the mouth of the cave into the open air of the main entrance as the mountain shuddered and crumbled around them. Upon what had once been the perch from which Boviss had surveyed his kingdom, those who had been his subjects gathered and waited. Fennecs and Reds huddled and tended to their wounds. The battle had not been without its casualties. Several had fallen. Several more were badly hurt. But most had survived. Sorrel and her young ones were among the last to emerge from the darkness. Though they had escaped the wrath of the dragon, the retreat had taken its toll on them. Falling debris and jagged broken floor had left the three of them battered, but they were in one piece.

"Well?" asked Sorrel as a handful of malthropes hurried to help her.

"In all, we lost twenty," said the Fennec chieftain. "Twelve of ours, eight of the Reds."

"Twenty is twenty," she said. "The rest doesn't matter. We are one. Remember this."

"And the dragon?"

"He was caught. The chain held. That is all I know. But the mountain has stopped shaking." She held out a hand. "A torch."

One of the Reds handed her a light and sparked it to life.

"Who will go with me? After what we have done, I will not leave until I know I will not be followed."

The others looked to one another. One by one, the most able-bodied of the remaining malthropes took up torches. Fifty of them, including both chieftains, followed Sorrel back through the tunnels. What had once been a masterpiece of dwarven architecture lay in utter ruin. The farther into the lair they crept, the less remained of the carvings and columns. It was a jagged mess now. The mountain had reclaimed it. With the care of creatures all-too-familiar with the threat that may yet breathe within these tunnels, they crept deeper. Over rubble and between great slabs they climbed until they reached the chamber where the trap had been set. What had once been a tall, empty chamber was now a massive mound of stone. Here and there, hints of scaly hide could be seen between the piles of fallen mountain. As they drew near, something beneath the rubble shifted. A few stones fell away. It was enough to reveal a single eye peering out from beneath the pile.

Boviss had survived, but only just. He took labored breaths. Licks of weak flame curled from between stones. The floor was wet with pools of dark, potent blood.

"He clings to life," the forest chieftain murmured. "For now."

The Fennec chieftain turned to Sorrel. "Should we end him? We can take up the weapons, hack at him until he draws his last breath."

"Or we can leave him here and let him wither as he would have withered us," the forest chieftain offered. "What say you?"

"Why do you ask me this?" Sorrel asked.

"You led us this far. You freed us from him," the forest chieftain said.

"We, in all our time, could not do such a thing," her desert counterpart added.

"So you expect me to lead you?" Sorrel said.

"I can think of no one better suited. The times ahead will be trying. We must rebuild. And you bring with you precious knowledge from far off lands," said the forest chieftain.

"I bring with me common sense that you should have as well." Sorrel sighed and looked to her young. "What do you think?"

"Us, Mama?" Wren said.

"You're asking *us* what we should do?" added Reyna.

"Why shouldn't I? I rescued the villagers, but you rescued me. And besides, you won the game, didn't you? You deserve your reward."

The twins looked to one another. They whispered back and forth.

"You still owe us a story, right?" Wren asked.

Sorrel smiled. "Of course. Though I don't know if I can dream up an adventure for Swift that is better than what you've done here."

"We didn't have to deal with Boviss very long," Reyna said. "The villagers had to deal with him a lot longer, so we think they should decide."

"But if they won't, we think that killing Boviss is much better than what Boviss has done to them. He made them suffer for years. Made them work for him."

"We think Boviss should do the same," Reyna said.

"We already took his hoard. But he's got a *lot* more to pay back than that."

The Story of Sorrel

"It could be dangerous," Sorrel said. "Are you sure?"

"We beat him before. And what's left of him after this? We can do it again."

Sorrel turned to the chieftains. "It would be the cruelest punishment we could muster, I think. If cruelty is what you seek."

"I do not desire cruelty," the forest chieftain said. "But justice…"

"Yes," the Fennec agreed. "Justice."

"Then you have your answer. But I leave it to you." She crouched and hugged her little ones. "I have a good long story to tell. And after that, a good long sleep."

#

The weeks and months to follow were anything but simple. The village of Gall, home to the Red malthropes, was largely in ruin. Burrow hadn't fared much better. Years of endless rivalry had built walls between the hearts and minds of the natives of the desert and the forest, but necessity had thrust them back together to scratch their way back from the wreckage that Boviss's wrath had made of their homes. The bountiful hunting grounds around Gall, for the first time, fed both the Fennecs and the Reds. In exchange, the desert malthropes brought their expertise in metal and stone. Damage that might have taken years to clear and repair without the proper tools was corrected in the space of a single season. The communities, once joined, were truly stronger than they had ever been apart.

Though she and her brood were unquestionably the agents of this sweeping and long-overdue change, Sorrel was the slowest to adjust. She'd spent her life on the move. Every skill she had was built upon the expectation that she could rely upon no one but herself. And now she was with her kind. Now she was surrounded by hearts and minds so like hers, and yet so different. Some nights she found herself seated in the mouth of her own burrow, eyes set on the open forest to the north, asking herself if this was truly what she wanted. Something called upon her to continue, to retreat to the wretched life that she had become comfortable with. Always her mind shifted back to her young ones. She'd thought she'd seen joy on their faces before. When they got a proper meal. When they heard a stirring adventure of their beloved Swift. But when she watched them now, she realized that what they'd felt then was a shadow of what they felt now. Running and jumping with others their age. Playing. Not some "game" that was a veiled lesson on the cruelty of the world, but a genuine game. They hid, they climbed, they tagged. And if they failed? No finger across the throat to warn them of the consequences. Simply another game and another chance to win.

In time, as her young grew stronger, and she grew older, she found her gaze lingering instead toward the south. The Reds and Fennecs had combined their villages into a place they called Den. It sat at the southern fringe of the forest, overlooking the desert where the Fennecs did their best work, and flanked by the thicker woods where the Reds thrived. Beyond the sandy dunes lay another thin forest. And beyond that, South Crescent. Sorrel and the twins were the only ones who had truly been there. Indeed, Sorrel and the twins were the only ones who had ever had to deal with a world that elves, humans, and the like called their own. Season after season, she watched for the signs. Wisps of smoke on the horizon. The sails of boats bobbing on the waves. The world of man and elf drawing nearer, now that Boviss no longer darkened the skies. The challenge of the dragon was behind them now, but other challenges lay ahead.

Years later, when the people of South Crescent were growing ever bolder, it seemed inevitable that there would come a clash every bit as bloody as the one with Boviss. On that day, a new solution presented itself. Like Boviss, it was safety that came at a terrible price. But that is a story for another time.

From The Author

Thank you for reading! If you liked this story, or perhaps if you found it lacking, I'd love to hear from you. You can find my social media, my email, and my newsletter at:

www.bookofdeacon.com/contact

Discover other titles by Joseph R. Lallo:

The Book of Deacon Series:

Book 1: *The Book of Deacon*
Book 2: *The Great Convergence*
Book 3: *The Battle of Verril*
Book 4: *The D'Karon Apprentice*
Book 5: *The Crescents*

Other stories in the same setting:

Jade
The Rise of the Red Shadow
The Redemption of Desmeres

The Big Sigma Series:

Book 1: *Bypass Gemini*
Book 2: *Unstable Prototypes*
Book 3: *Artificial Evolution*
Book 4: *Temporal Contingency*
Book 5: *Temporal Contingency*

The Free-Wrench Series:

Book 1: *Free-Wrench*
Book 2: *Skykeep*
Book 3: *Ichor Well*
Book 4: *The Calderan Problem*
Book 5: *Cipher Hill*